"I've missed you, sweetheart."

Brad spoke his false affection just loudly enough for the press to hear, then pulled Gail toward him, pressing his lips against hers in a long, passionate kiss that left Gail's pulse racing.

"No questions tonight, gang," he told the reporters. "I'm going home to be alone with my bride."

Brad maintained a hold on Gail until they were completely alone. "How dare you show up here unannounced. You could've jeopardized my whole campaign!" She could see the anger in his eyes.

"Brad, I just thought—never mind what I thought." How could she explain that while their marriage might be a farce, her feelings for him were anything but?

Kate Denton is a pseudonym for the writing team of Carolyn Hake and Jeanie Lambright. Both are Texans by adoption, Carolyn having come from Louisiana, Jeanie from Oklahoma. They work as specialists for the federal government in Health and Handicap Services (Carolyn) and Equal Employment Opportunity (Jeanie). Each has three children, and an assortment of cats and dogs! They are both history buffs and their hobbies include cooking, reading, old movies (Carolyn) and traveling, reading, ballet, and writing country and western song lyrics (Jeanie).

Winner Take All
Kate Denton

Harlequin Books

TORONTO • NEW YORK • LONDON
AMSTERDAM • PARIS • SYDNEY • HAMBURG
STOCKHOLM • ATHENS • TOKYO • MILAN

ISBN 0-373-02870-9

Harlequin Romance first edition November 1987

CHAPTER ONE

"NO, SAM. I won't do it. *No way.*"

"But he needs you, Gail."

"Oh no, he doesn't. A keeper maybe, but not me."

Her boss frowned. "Be serious now."

"I am serious. Really, Sam. The man's nothing but a spoiled, wealthy playboy. And the Western world's number one skirt chaser."

"Hardly the Western world." Sam leaned back in his chair, his lips twitching in a stifled smile.

"The United States and surrounding territories then."

"Come on, Gail. Just because some newspaper named him Bachelor of the Year doesn't automatically make him a playboy. Look at me. I'm a bachelor, remember?"

"You're different."

"I'm different, huh? Thanks for the compliment."

"Oh, you know what I mean. Quit putting words into my mouth."

"The only word I'm trying to put into your mouth is yes." Sam plucked a pipe from the wooden rack on his desk and began scraping the remnants of the bowl into the glass ashtray as he glowered at Gail. "Brad Harrison's in the race of his life for the Senate. He's got to pull enough votes to force a runoff. And you, Gail, could make that happen."

"Me? A mere legislative aide?" Gail shook her head. "How? From what I've read, the congressman from

Louisiana needs a lot more help than I could ever provide.'' She rose and paced the thick-carpeted floor in Sam's office.

"Don't go modest on me, Gail. You know you're more than just an aide. You've got a lot of political savvy. Experience, too. Not to mention your being a mighty fine-looking woman." He smiled, then cupped the bowl of his pipe and gestured toward Gail's pinstriped suit. "In spite of those brown and gray uniforms." His expression changed to a grimace.

Gail stopped pacing and turned to look at Sam. "Have we changed the subject? Just what does my wardrobe have to do with this conversation?''

"Sorry," he said, his face giving no hint of regret. "I'll get back to Brad, then. He does need your help, Gail. You know how to run a campaign office—how to get someone organized."

"Organization is one of Harrison's minor problems. Image is the major one." She walked over to the front of Sam's desk. "People don't want a party-animal for their senator. They want someone serious, hard working...."

"The way you go on," Sam chided, shaking his head. "Actually, this assignment could be good for you."

"Oh, in what way?" Gail wondered what he was getting at.

"Well, maybe after a few weeks with those young people over in the Harrison camp, you'd give up trying to look and act so much older than you are. Shed some of that protective coloration." He was eyeing her suit disapprovingly once more.

"There you go again," she said irritably. "Why don't you stop nagging me, Sam? I like wearing suits. They make me look professional. My father thought so, too."

"Balderdash! Your father, bless his soul, just never wanted you to play up your beauty. Then he'd have had to contend with a bunch of young men flocking around all the time. Would have lost his right arm."

"That's a bunch of nonsense, Sam. And you know it. And it's not going to sway me to change my position. I have no intention of playing baby-sitter to an overgrown teenager with runaway hormones."

"Okay, okay," Sam said with a loud sigh. He glanced at his watch. "Why don't you think on it for a while? Take a walk. Grab a sandwich. Then we'll talk some more. Maybe you'll be more receptive after lunch."

Gail eyed Sam warily, "I seriously doubt it. You're not smooth-talking me into this, Sam Wisterwood." She leaned onto Sam's desk. "But I will take that walk. You've been working me too hard this week. I'm going to enjoy a nice long lunch break."

"Good. And then I expect you to come back all ready to work for Brad Harrison."

"I told you before. No way." Gail turned on her heel and quickly headed out of the office.

Sam pulled out a black leather tobacco pouch from his top desk drawer and began filling his pipe. "She's just like her father," he muttered to himself. "Stubborn as a mule."

GAIL WASN'T the only one opposed to Sam's arrangement. Brad Harrison was just as obstinate. Sam had summoned the young congressman to his office soon after Gail had left. "Sam," Brad said decidedly, "I appreciate the offer, but frankly, this campaign's giving me enough trouble without my having to look after your little protégée."

Sam snorted. "Gail Meredith's a lot more than a protégée, Brad. Sure her dad was my best friend. Sure I hired her when he died. But Russell Meredith's daughter has crackerjack credentials. She managed my last campaign, and she just might be the key to your success. Anyway, what do you have to lose?"

"An election for one thing." Brad's tone was sarcastic.

"You seem to be doing a pretty good job of that on your own."

Brad groaned. He stretched out his long legs and leaned back in the chair, his hands clasped behind his head. "You're not one to mince words, are you Sam?" Brad's blue eyes were troubled, his thick blond brows almost fused together as he frowned at Sam. "The campaign is floundering—I'll be the first to admit that. But what more can I do? I'm working eighteen-hour days as it is, existing on a few hours of sleep, if that much. I'm not about to neglect my congressional duties while I campaign for the Senate. I can't afford to alienate the party by not appearing for crucial votes. And a campaign demands a full-time effort."

"That's exactly my point, Brad. That's why you need Gail Meredith. She'll help you pull the campaign together. Believe me." Sam obviously wasn't giving in.

Brad looked troubled—as if his mind was full of thoughts all pulling him in different directions. He gazed at Sam in resignation. "Okay," he sighed, "send her over. I'll find something for her to do."

"You don't need to sound so darned happy about it," Sam laughed. "It's not a punishment, you know. And for your information, she's as excited about the prospect as you are." Sam paused for effect taking an extra long puff at his pipe. "If I remember correctly, she referred to you as the skirt chaser of the Western world." Sam gave a half-smile cupping the bowl.

"Glad to hear she's got an open mind," Brad snapped. "Sounds like she's been listening to all those exaggerated stories about me. And believing them."

"Well, don't let it worry you, Brad. A little time with the Harrison campaign and Gail will realize that there's as much substance to you as there is style. And she'll help you convince the rest of the world that it's true."

Brad's face softened. His strong, square jaw unclenched. "Thanks, Sam—for the unexpected compliment." He ran his hand through his neat blow-dried hair. "Those are few and far between these days. What with my battles in the House of Representatives and now the campaign troubles, sometimes I think my aunt and my public relations manager are the only ones who have ever had anything good to say about me." A sad, cynical smile appeared on his lips, then quickly disappeared.

Sam came around the desk and clasped Brad on the shoulder. "That bad, huh? Campaign must be getting really rough."

"Like a hurricane brewing in the Gulf of Mexico." Brad gave a half smile. "And I'm out in a leaky boat."

"All the more reason to get you some help. And Gail might just end up being your lifesaver."

"Well, I set myself up for that, didn't I?"

"Yep," Sam laughed. "You sure did. So now that we're agreed on Gail's helping you, I guess you two should meet as soon as possible. I'll bring her to the reception tonight. We'll see you then." He shook Brad's hand firmly.

Sam eased his rotund frame back into the leather chair behind his desk as he watched Brad leave the office. He took a puff on his ever-present pipe and smiled. "One down, one to go," he muttered, then noticed Gail passing by his door on the way to her office. He rose and motioned her in. "Brad Harrison was here. You just missed him."

"Pity," she said flippantly.

"I see your walk didn't mellow you."

"Not a bit."

"Too bad. That's one of the things I can usually count on with you, Gail. You don't stay mad long."

"I wasn't mad," Gail said, following Sam back into his office. "Just determined. This time, Senator Wisterwood, you're not going to get your way."

"Do I ever?" Sam tapped his pipe into the glass ashtray, seemingly fascinated by the contents spilling out. He pulled out his tobacco pouch again as Gail stood by impatiently. Sam used his pipe as a stage prop—to create the effect of being eminently wise, somehow, and his machinations amused Gail.

"You know you do, Sam. But not this time. As I told you—"

"Not now," Sam interrupted. He put up a hand to stop any more words. "I'm due for a roll call, then I've got to study that speech you're writing. Just keep thinking about what I said. By the way, while you're thinking, I want you to attend a reception with me tonight. A reception for Brad. Melva'll give you the details." Sam smoothed his sparse gray hairs and adjusted his tie. "Gotta go. Pick you up at eight."

"Okay, run out," Gail called after him, "but my mind's made up. And I'm not going to any reception."

The door slamming behind him was Sam's response.

GAIL STARED into her closet. It was six-thirty. That darned Sam. Wasting half her day lobbying on behalf of Brad Harrison and now dragging her to a reception. What should she wear? She had planned on staying home and doing her laundry. She wasn't even sure she had anything clean to put on. It would serve Sam right if she were still in her bathrobe when he arrived. She slid several hangers across the rack bemoaning her sparse wardrobe. She knew it was her own fault. But she'd always told herself it was useless spending good money for clothes, especially evening dresses, considering her social life—or lack of social life would be more like it. She spied the brown silk shirtwaist dress. It would do. She could fancy it up with pearls.

Gail moved to the bathroom and stepped into the steamy tub she'd filled a few minutes before. She stretched out and leaned back, trying to relax and rid herself of the image stuck in her brain.

Brad Harrison. Sam's idea was appalling. She had no respect for the man at all. From everything she'd heard, he was more a womanizer than legislator, his main pursuits being to cram as many cocktail parties as possible into his life and to pose, usually with nubile young females, for newspaper pictures. Gail realized a lot of high-level negotiations took place in social settings, but she had little respect for the cocktail party crowd. She doubted that anyone who was a daily feature in the gossip columns, as was Congressman Harrison, could manage much serious business no matter where he was.

Gail grabbed a tube of shampoo, drained the bath and turned on the shower. So much for soaking and for wasting time on thoughts of the congressman. Or on Sam Wisterwood's preposterous idea for her to join the Harrison bandwagon. It was asking too much that she give up an evening to the doomed campaign. Enough was enough.

Twenty minutes later, a frustrated Gail was glaring through her glasses at her reflection in the mirror. A conspiracy was at work here. First, the hem had worked loose from her dress and she'd had to secure it with transparent tape. Then her freshly shampooed hair had resisted all coaxing into a more stylish upsweep. Finally Gail had given up, thrown down her brush and pulled her long hair back into its usual ponytail.

She heard a taxi door slam. No time for any more primping tonight. Gail disliked it anyway. She had never spent much time on her appearance. Besides, she thought, the result was always the same—sweet. If she'd been told once, she'd been told a hundred times, "Gail, you have such a sweet face." Every time she heard it, she gritted her teeth. Sweet was just a synonym for plain, she thought.

She took a final glance in the full-length mirror. Still unimpressive, she mused. More angles, fewer curves—that's what she needed—and what she wouldn't give for another few inches to add to her five-foot-one frame. I look about sixteen tonight, she thought, *sweet* sixteen. "What's the use?" she asked herself, shrugging her shoulders and sighing. Gail still saw herself as an overweight teenager, though she'd long since grown out of that. Beneath the glasses and the conservative clothes was a pretty woman—one with unusually large brown eyes, dark blond hair and a beautiful warm smile.

Sam's knock sounded at the door as she grabbed her purse and turned out the light.

The taxi lurched to a stop in front of a white stone mansion with a large portico. "Obviously Brad Harrison has some well-heeled admirers," Gail whispered to Sam as they walked up the stairs toward the ornate entranceway. "Some crusty old magnate from New Orleans?"

"You'll see soon enough," Sam answered.

The pair was ushered inside to a large marbled hall where a receiving line awaited them. Gail recognized Congressman Harrison immediately. The handsome blonde was nodding as he greeted guests. He wore a classic black tuxedo, and as with all politicians, a trained smile was in place, accompanied by a firm two-handed handshake. But this man had embellished his act with eye signals. Was Gail imagining it, or was he sending each woman a private message?

Gail and Sam approached the receiving line. "Hello, Judith," Sam greeted the woman standing on Brad's left. "I don't believe you've met Gail Meredith. Gail, our hostess, Judith DeWitt."

A smooth-skinned enchantress, Judith was sophisticated, tall, the kind of awesome beauty that made other females feel like gawky adolescents. The woman turned to face Gail, looking her over quickly and then gave her an odd smile. Gail wasn't sure what the woman meant by it, but she did sense that she felt Gail represented no competition. Small wonder. Gail felt just the opposite—this was a lady to be reckoned with. She seemed to have everything that Gail did not. Gail's feelings of inadequacy were intensified as Brad turned to smile at Judith. To Gail, he seemed a man bewitched. In a minute he would be drooling. His attention turned to Sam. "Hey, Sam," Brad began, glancing at the senator, "I'm glad you could make it." Then his eyes and smile focused on Gail. "And is every beautiful woman in Washington here tonight?" he said as his hands wrapped around Gail's, squeezing it warmly.

Gail wanted to feel irritation at his falsely flattering greeting, but her mind and body weren't in concert. She knew he probably greeted everyone he met with the same sort of affection, yet his touch still disturbed her in an undefinable way. What was the man trying to do—seduce every woman in sight? She had half a mind to tell him just what she thought of his playboy tactics. But when she raised her face up to his and locked stares with those caressing blue eyes, all resistance faded.

"Brad, this is Gail Meredith."

"Sam," he said, eyes still focused on Gail, "you disappoint me. When you were telling me about Ms Meredith, you failed to mention how pretty she is." He surveyed her almost seductively.

Gail pulled her hand away from Brad. "Is that a qualification for working on the Harrison campaign, Congressman?" she asked dryly, her anger finally surfacing. Who did he think he was, trying to con her with his uninspired compliments?

"Not necessarily a qualification," he winked at her, "but it sure makes coming to work nicer when there are some good-looking women in the office." He squeezed her elbow as he adroitly moved her along. "Now why don't you join the others and enjoy some of Judith's special punch? We'll talk some more later."

The punch sounded like a good idea to Gail. She felt flushed, maybe even a little lightheaded. They must have turned up the heat tonight. Sam put a hand gently on her back as they passed into the living room to mingle. The crowd was very elegantly dressed.

Sam seemed to know everyone. They each got a cup of bourbon punch and as Sam chatted with various guests, Gail placed herself against a wall where she could unobtrusively get a second view of Judith and Brad.

She eyed the hostess's long flowing dress—a black chiffon creation covered by a beaded tunic. The black of her outfit enhanced Judith's dark beauty, her shiny blue-black hair and brilliant onyx eyes. She was devastatingly attractive. Not only that—she was rich too. Her home was evidence of that. According to Sam, it was only a small part of a healthy divorce settlement Judith had received several years before.

But Gail's envious gaze was drawn from Judith to the man beside her. The newspaper photographs certainly hadn't done him justice. They had never captured the vibrant blue of his eyes nor the golden highlights of his sun-streaked hair. His height—he looked to be about six foot four—surprised her. No wonder he always seemed to tower over women. Any woman Gail's height would have to stand on tiptoe even to get the top of her head into a shot with him. Her heart raced involuntarily as she remembered their brief encounter in the reception line. The mere grip of his handshake had made her whole body tingle with warmth. And he knew it. He must have. It was probably just the kind of reaction he'd wanted her to have. Their encounter only confirmed her opinion. The man was a playboy, and would be impossible to work for. She stole another glance at the reception line, only to meet those vivid blue eyes head-on again. Was he watching her? Ridiculous. He just knew how to make every female think she was the only woman in the room. If Congressman Harrison had as much skill at politics as he had at eye and body language, he wouldn't be needing assistance on his campaign.

"Hiding?" Sam walked up to Gail carrying two fresh cups of punch. She set her empty cup on a nearby table and accepted Sam's offering.

"No, not hiding. Observing."

"And just who are you observing?" Sam smiled knowingly. "The young congressman across the room, perhaps?"

"Yes. I'm also wondering why you're so anxious to send me off on such an obvious suicide mission. I don't want to spend the next few months working my hindquarters off for that gorgeous lout standing across the room flashing all those teeth."

"You think he's gorgeous?"

"Give the devil his due," Gail admitted. "He seems to have quite a flair for small talk. All the ladies appear captivated."

"What about the men?"

"They can't get through for the crush of women waiting their turn." Gail didn't want to admit to Sam that she'd been watching Brad Harrison ever since they'd arrived and that the men did seem almost as captivated by him as the women. They listened with an interest and respect that appeared real. But it likely wasn't as it seemed. He probably was reciting some well-practiced greeting to each guest. Something put together by an overworked, underpaid staffer. "The man probably couldn't put three sentences together without a speech writer feeding him his lines," Gail muttered cynically.

After all the guests had gone through the receiving line and drained at least two cups of punch, Judith moved to the center of the large arched doorway and rang a silver bell. "Attention, everyone," she said in a dramatic voice befitting her appearance. "It's time that we heard from our guest of honor, our future United States Senator, Congressman Bradley Harrison."

There was enthusiastic applause as Brad moved to the center of the archway, smiled, and nodded his appreciation. "Ladies and gentlemen, I want to thank you all for coming tonight. Now, I'm not going to bore you with a long political speech—" There was light applause and some congenial laughter. Brad laughed, too. "But I want to stress again the most important issue facing this campaign—environmental protection.

"Most of you know my main opponent—Merton Ramsey." The crowd let out a few boos. Brad smiled. "Can't say I disagree with you. Merton Ramsey is a menace—a thorn in the side of all those committed to this cause.

"As a senator, Ramsey would be in a position to focus on the legislative needs of the conglomerates. And would we be surprised when he did?"

"No!" they chorused.

"That's right. We can't afford to forget that he was president of South Louisiana Oil. The same people who brought us the Gulf of Mexico's largest oil spill. Is this the kind of man we want representing the people's needs? The kind of man to protect our environment?"

The crowd shouted more no's.

"Then I'm asking you to help me." Brad went on to explain his concerns and the solutions he would bring about.

The group listened with interest. Gail was fascinated, not just by the image in the doorway—the tall attractive man with the wheat-colored hair and electric-blue eyes. No—it was more than that. What Brad was saying had real meaning. Surprisingly, she found she agreed with his concerns and marveled at his proposals. Maybe she had underestimated this man. Maybe he wasn't just a facade, a windup Washington mannequin, after all.

The group exploded into loud clapping when Brad finished, and supporters thronged around the candidate. She wished she could get closer to Brad, tell him how she felt about his ideas, but it was impossible. Aside from the party loyalists, there was the adoring female contingent pushing in for a few more seconds with the man of the hour.

Gail hadn't really expected another encounter with Congressman Harrison and was surprised to see him making his way across the room toward her and Sam. His progress was slow since he paused several times to chat with fawning females. Gail didn't need to read lips to get the gist of those conversations. The innuendo was clear just by watching his expressive face—a nod, a wink, that knock-em-dead smile.

"Sorry we haven't had more time to talk," Brad said glancing at his watch when he finally joined Sam and Gail. "I didn't realize it was so late. I feel like a robot the way I've been moving around." He sighed with fatigue as his eyes surveyed the large crowd of supporters.

He sure was smooth for a robot, Gail thought. Were they supposed to feel sorry for him because he was working so hard at seducing every woman in sight? She raised long silky eyelashes to look up disbelievingly at Brad. But he did look tired—exhausted as a matter of fact, though it made him no less attractive.

"Hang in there, my boy," Sam encouraged. "It was a good little speech."

"Was it? Sometimes I wonder. Maybe I should give up on this quixotic effort. Is it worth it?"

"Sure it is," Sam answered. "Just picture Merton Ramsey waving his arms in a signal of victory. Think of him representing Louisiana in the Senate."

"Over my dead body," Brad responded. "And the way I feel tonight, that's a distinct possibility. Let's face it, I need a miracle."

"Maybe that's just what we can deliver," Sam said.

Gail shot daggers at Sam, but he averted his eyes from hers as he clasped Brad on the shoulder. "Gail will talk to you about that in the morning."

"Yes, and the morning will be here soon if we're not careful." Gail was irked. "Let's go, Sam." She turned, heading for the door leaving Sam to bid Brad a hasty goodbye.

Gail and Sam rode quietly in the taxi until Sam broke the silence. "Well, are you convinced the man has some substance now that you've heard what he has to say? Are you willing to go to work for Brad?"

Gail sighed loudly. "To tell you the truth, Sam, I was impressed with what he said and how he said it. Really impressed. But I also like working for you and frankly I still don't really see how I could help him. I'll admit he looks imposing as a candidate. But from what I read in the newspapers, he'll need a lot more than the likes of me could provide." She watched as Sam pulled his pipe from his coat pocket.

He tapped it into the ashtray. "And just what have you been seeing in the paper, young lady?"

"The same thing as everyone else—'The Lives and Loves of Brad Harrison.' Tonight I saw him in action with my own eyes. He was practically flirting with every woman at the reception, me included. Sam, I couldn't work for someone so unorthodox."

"Since when is liking pretty women unorthodox?" Sam cocked an eyebrow. "Women do vote, you know."

"Yes, but making a career of flirtation when there's serious work to be done, isn't exactly going to endear him to the voters."

"You're probably right about that. Ramsey's certain to make the most of Brad's playboy image." He shook his head resignedly.

Gail looked at Sam. "Besides, what's all this to you? Party politics aside, why are you so concerned about Brad Harrison?"

"I just see a bright young man with a lot to offer."

"A lot to offer whom?" she asked. "You mean the voters?"

"Of course the voters. Who else would I mean?" Sam turned his head to stare out the window. A long silence ensued, then he turned to her. "Gail, one of these days you won't have me around to look out for you. Sure you've got a lot going for you—a master's degree and a Phi Beta Kappa key. But you've got to do more to establish yourself in Washington and this is a good opportunity. I think Brad Harrison is going to be around a long time. He's got that special something. It's not a bad star to hitch your wagon to."

"Hmmm." Gail eyed him warily.

"Look," Sam said. "I've arranged for you to meet with him at nine o'clock tomorrow morning. Go on over to his office. Talk to him. Once you get to know the guy—know more about what he stands for, you'll feel different."

"I doubt it," she grumbled.

"My Aunt Agnes. You're one exasperating woman. As pigheaded as they come."

"That's the pot calling the kettle black, isn't it, you stubborn old coot?"

"Yes—" he chuckled "—I guess it is." He opened the taxi door to let her out. "Good night, Gail." He stepped back into the taxi and rolled down the window. "And don't think I'll be anything but stubborn about this." The taxi waited until Gail had walked up the steps to her apartment, then sped off into the night.

That crafty old Sam, she thought, entering the building. He knew her all too well. She couldn't imagine any career other than politics and yet, she'd never really thought of the future, of what she would do if something happened to Sam. She'd always had confidence in her professional credentials, but now the truth hit home. The time had come to establish her worth without family or friendship to rely on. If she did contribute to Brad Harrison's defeat of Merton Ramsey, it would not only be a feather in Brad's hat, but in hers as well.

Not for the first time in her life, Gail longed for a mother or a best friend, someone to help her weigh the pros and cons of this decision. But her mother had died when she was an infant. She had no close friends—except Sam.

The public arena had been a way of life for Gail since childhood. All through her teen years she'd helped out on her father's campaigns, worked on projects and was always involved in the political scene in one way or another. Russell Meredith loved to brag that his daughter was a born "pol." It never occurred to him that this one-dimensional upbringing might cause her to miss out on other experiences. He never noticed she was not doing what other girls her age were—dating, primping, gossiping about boys, talking about clothes. Gail had become preoccupied with politics to the exclusion of everything else, and neither she nor her father realized this at the time.

Gail would sometimes lie in bed at night and reflect on her cloistered existence and her lack of personal life. She would regret the absence of a special man, of a family in her world. But exhausted sleep would usually bring such thoughts to a halt. And the next day she'd be too busy, too enmeshed in her career to continue her musing of the night before.

GAIL STARED at the sign on the door. Congressman Bradley Harrison III, State of Louisiana. Below it hung a round congressional seal. She took a deep breath and turned the knob. "Hello," she greeted the receptionist sitting in the anteroom. "I'm Gail Meredith. I believe Congressman Harrison is expecting me."

The receptionist, an attractive woman in her forties, looked at Gail with surprise. "I'm sorry, Miss Meredith. I'm afraid the congressman's not in yet."

"Well, I'm sure he's expecting me," Gail protested. She eyed a sofa against the wall, "I'll just sit over here and wait."

The minutes ticked by slowly. Gail sat on the couch, her legs crossed, one foot jiggling nervously. She glanced repeatedly at her watch. She looked up expectantly as the office door opened. But it was not Brad. It was a younger man in his late twenties, she guessed.

"Hi, Phyllis," he said, addressing the receptionist. "What's on Brad's agenda for today?"

Gail couldn't hear the response but the receptionist gestured toward her so she knew they were discussing her. The young man walked toward her smiling, his hand extended. "Hi, I'm Dave McElroy. Can I be of assistance?" He sat in the armchair next to the couch.

Gail liked him immediately. His friendly smile and warm Southern accent made her feel at ease. Why was she so uptight anyway? She was here to do the congressman a favor. There was nothing to be so on edge about. He probably had a perfectly good excuse for being a little late. Washington traffic was horrendous. "Glad to meet you," she replied sincerely. "I'm Gail Meredith and I'm here to discuss my working on Congressman Harrison's campaign."

"Oh, really?" Dave seemed surprised. "Well that's good news. Brad needs all the help he can get this time out. He told me he was going to get another man. I guess I didn't realize help would come in the form of a woman—a pretty one at that." He rose from the chair. "I wish I had more time, Gail, but I've got some urgent phone calls to make. Maybe I'll see you before you leave."

Gail felt the same irritation she'd felt with his boss. "Pretty" indeed. These Louisiana men seemed to scatter compliments around like confetti. She could feel her body begin to tense again. She looked at the clock on the wall. Nine-thirty. "Do you think the congressman will be in shortly?" she asked Dave.

"I'm sure something unexpected came up," he mumbled, turning to the receptionist. "Phyllis, take care of our visitor while she waits for the congressman. Gotta get to those calls now." He disappeared into an office.

For over an hour Gail sat sipping black coffee and reading *Newsweek* magazine, both provided by Phyllis. Her irritation was growing minute by minute, and she had half a mind to call Sam and tell him what she thought of this assignment and party loyalty.

She had become tired of reading and had just begun pacing the floor, wondering whether she should leave when the door opened and Brad Harrison entered—dressed in the same black tux he'd worn to the reception. It was obvious he hadn't been home. He stopped by Phyllis's desk and she gestured toward Gail. He had just started walking her way when the outer door opened again and a group of women entered. Constituents, no doubt. He stopped and flashed his pat politician's smile, chatting for several moments before instructing Phyllis to provide the passes they had requested. Finally, he made his way to Gail.

"Ms Meredith. You look a lot fresher than I do." The familiar smile he seemed to turn on and off like a light was missing as he addressed Gail. "Sorry I'm late. I was meeting with some fund-raisers from Louisiana and the meeting lasted longer than I expected. A lot longer. Lucky I keep an extra suit at the office. I live in Georgetown and you'd have been even more upset with me if I'd gone all the way home to shower and change."

Fund-raisers, my foot, thought Gail as she shook his hand. More like hell-raising. This was impossible. Just as she knew it would be. Why did she let Sam bamboozle her into considering this job? She let out a soft unintelligible sigh as she bent to retrieve her purse from the floor.

Brad looked down at Gail, and every ounce of his politician's training couldn't hide his dismay. "Will you excuse me for one more minute?" he asked Gail as Dave reappeared in the reception area. Brad pulled him aside. "Can you believe this is the pro Sam promised us—this little half-pint? I could hardly hide my shock last night. She's going to save my campaign?" he whispered.

Dave shrugged his shoulders noncommittally.

"Sam must be losing it." Brad went on, "To foist someone like this on us—is like sending ice to the Titanic. Now what am I going to do?"

"Don't ask me—you're the boss," Dave answered. "Besides she might be just what we need. Give her a chance."

"Thanks. You're a big help, Dave. All I need is another problem. She's so vulnerable looking, I feel I should be the rescuer, not she." Dave shrugged again and headed into his office.

Brad's look was somber as he turned back to Gail.

"I desperately need a cup of coffee. Can I get you one Gail?"

"No thanks," she answered. "That one I had was strong enough to last me all week."

Brad laughed. "Ah yes, Louisiana's finest chicory coffee." He winked at Phyllis. "It does take a bit of getting used to. But after you've had a cup or two, you'll be refusing to drink that watery liquid the rest of America calls coffee."

That'll be the day, Gail thought. Not only did it taste dreadful, it was probably fattening too. She followed Brad into his office and took a chair facing his desk. Brad walked around and seated himself in a plush leather chair. He leaned back, as relaxed as if he were accustomed to wearing a tuxedo in the office all the time. Maybe there had been lots of nights when he didn't go home, Gail decided as she watched him.

Brad was also studying her as he stirred his coffee. Gail wondered what was going on in his head. Was he questioning whether she could really be as competent—as smart—as the Arkansas senator had bragged? Sometimes Gail wondered herself. Although she always appreciated Sam's support, she knew he was biased where she was concerned. The congressman propped an elbow on the desk and continued watching her. His look was disconcerting. She'd heard the term "bedroom eyes" but had never before appreciated the expression. She felt the need to cross her arms over her breasts, to somehow protect herself from his piercing inspection. It took effort to restrain herself.

"I don't bite."

"What?"

"Well, you're sitting there like an errant schoolgirl, your hands neatly folded in your lap."

Gail quickly moved one hand to the arm of her chair. This wasn't going to work. She was becoming more certain of that by the minute. Oh well, she'd go through the pretense of an interview and then tell Sam thanks but no thanks. This time she'd make Sam accept her refusal. Brad Harrison was examining her as if she were Little Miss Muffet and he were the spider.

"Sam says you're unexcited about the prospect of working for me." His eyes seemed to be flashing in amusement.

Gail was uncomfortable. She didn't realize Sam had shared her reluctance with Brad—and just how much had he shared? Brad seemed to be enjoying himself immensely at her expense. Gail also got the impression she wasn't particularly wanted by the Harrison camp. It wasn't anything precise that made her feel that way, nothing she could put her finger on. It was just a feeling. Gail never had been adventurous, but this was suddenly becoming interesting, a game of wills. Maybe she would take the job after all . . . if for nothing more than to show that handsome Don Juan across the desk from her that she was a bright, competent woman.

CHAPTER TWO

"Now, Gail," Brad said. "May I call you Gail? As Sam told you, should we come to terms you would be in charge of my campaign in Louisiana. Sam speaks very highly of your skills." While his tone was conciliatory, his expression was hard to read, and Gail still had to wonder what he really thought about all this.

"I've got satellite offices in Alexandria, Shreveport and Monroe. With the main office in New Orleans. Of course, we keep a small group here in Washington. So you would be commuting between all those places."

He picked up a thick folder and handed it to her. "This is a voter profile. It'll also give you some demographic information." He shoved the report across the desk to her.

As Gail skimmed the pages, Brad rose from his chair and walked toward the window. She found her eyes following him. He flexed his shoulders and she thought his muscles must be tense. For some reason she imagined her hands soothing them. Obviously his late hours were getting the best of him, she decided. This was confirmed by a smothered yawn. What was wrong with her, she wondered, collecting her wits just as he turned around.

"Any questions?" he asked, gesturing toward the report.

"Well...er," Gail stammered. "Not yet." Gail quickly scanned the rest of the report and was surprised by the quality of the work, the detail, the organization. Good staff effort, she thought.

They began discussing the report. As they talked, Gail found her mind wandering again. She couldn't help but notice how attractive and desirable he looked, leaning back in his chair, bow tie undone and thick golden hair slightly mussed, hanging over his forehead. Her thoughts were interrupted by the telephone.

"Oh, Judith. Long time no see." He laughed. "Me too. My cuff links?" He looked at both his wrists and laughed even louder as he viewed the missing links. "Yep, they're mine, all right."

Gail was exasperated. This was impossible. No wonder his campaign was in trouble. He probably hadn't spent a single minute campaigning. He was clearly too busy playing house with gullible women. Quality reports by dedicated staff didn't mean a hill of beans if the man up front wasn't committed. Her first instincts had been correct.

After five more minutes of shallow chit-chat and conspiratorial laughter, Brad ended the conversation. He then dialed another number. "Phyllis," he said, "no more calls—unless it's the president needing some advice." He grinned and winked at Gail.

"Now, Ms Meredith." His mood suddenly became serious. "Tell me about yourself."

Gail wasn't prepared for that. She thought they had been discussing the campaign plans, not Gail Meredith. "Just what would you like to know?" she replied skeptically.

"The usual. Your background, your qualifications for this position. Did you bring a résumé?" Brad was leaning forward on the desk, arms crossed. She felt as if his eyes were drilling into her.

"Um—ah," she stumbled, then suddenly she was angry. What was going on here anyway? "Congressman," she began, her professional poise returning, "my understanding was that Senator Wisterwood was offering my services to your campaign for a few months and that we were here to discuss that possibility. I had assumed you were briefed on my background and qualifications. But as a matter of information—" Gail went on to outline her educational and professional credentials.

"But do you have any campaign experience other than for your father and Senator Wisterwood," he prodded.

"Are you questioning my ability, Congressman? I should think Senator Wisterwood's recommendation satisfactory. But if that isn't the case, and if the credentials I've shared aren't adequate, maybe we shouldn't waste more of your valuable time. Besides, I'm sure you need to get back to your adoring public."

"Just what do you mean by that?" Brad stood up.

"Just what I said. Your phone conversation a few moments ago tells me a lot about your commitment to serious campaigning. You're more interested in fun and games." Gail stood up to leave.

"Judgmental little thing, aren't you?" One eyebrow shot up in a challenging stare.

"Perhaps I am judgmental, Congressman. That's one of the things Sam Wisterwood pays me for—to use common sense and good judgment." She met Brad's stare. "And my good judgment and the polls I've been reading tell me your campaign is in dire need of those qualities."

"Maybe so," Brad admitted. "But they don't need to be accompanied by large doses of narrow-mindedness. You remind me of one of my old high school teachers—a spinster who relieved her frustrations by criticizing others."

Gail opened her mouth but could generate no reply. She simply grabbed her purse and briefcase and fled. She raced back toward the Dirksen Building. She was furious. Mainly with herself. One thing for sure, she was too disturbed to go back to work. She needed a walk and fresh air to cool off. Brad Harrison had made her mad. Who was he to treat her like that? He was impossible. First he insinuated she couldn't handle the job, then he acted as if Sam had been foisting her off on him, and finally he insulted her. Worst of all, despite her better judgment, despite her conviction that he was simply a womanizer, she had been drawn to him and had found him attractive. That made her even more livid.

She simply couldn't go back to the office and deal with Sam's questions. Not yet. She changed course and began walking around the Capitol grounds, hoping to pound her anger and confusion into the pavement. Her interview with the congressman was a washout and had definitely added insult to injury. Here she was, reluctantly subjecting herself to the possibility of assisting this pseudolegislator and his campaign, and he'd had the nerve to question her ability. To imply she was...she was—Oh, what was she going to tell Sam? One thing for sure, she wasn't going to work for Brad Harrison.

Gail took a deep breath as she gazed toward the Washington Monument. She wished she could really appreciate the view before her. Spring was already displaying its dazzling colors. Cherry blossoms and azaleas had burst into bloom, offering an array of fresh whites and soft pinks. The trees, too, were coming alive, their new leaves swaying in the mild breeze.

The same breeze pulled wisps of dark blond hair from Gail's long ponytail. Irritatedly, she brushed the hair off her face. The beauty surrounding her was doing nothing to restore her equilibrium. She wished now she'd told that pompous ill-mannered jerk just what she thought of him.

Gail turned and headed inside the Capitol building. She took her usual series of detours and passages. But she was in no mood today to take the time to go into the House and Senate Chambers for a quick update. Instead, she hurried to the basement, where she caught the underground shuttle to the Dirksen Building. She exited from the shuttle, headed to the elevators and pushed the Up button impatiently, grateful when the sluggish doors finally opened. Her momentum was fueled by her anger. Sam's ears ought to be burning by now if there was anything to mental telepathy.

Gail stalked into Sam's office and stopped short. His ears were burning all right. He was surrounded by a group of irate constituents—a poultry delegation from Little Rock. They were complaining loudly about the recent rise in feed prices. After catching Sam's eye Gail turned and headed toward her office. She'd have to wait her turn with Sam, and from the looks of it he'd probably be busy for quite a while.

But Sam hadn't become Arkansas' most successful senator on his looks. He was a born negotiator. Within ten minutes, Gail could hear happy chatter and promises of support in the next election as the group departed. A confident Sam appeared in her doorway, his round face decorated with a satisfied grin. "That was fun," he said. "Nice bunch of people. So come on in my office and tell me what you and Brad decided." He disappeared from the doorway.

Gail waited for a couple of minutes, then calmly entered his office and took the chair in front of his desk.

Sam watched her closely as he waited for her report. But she sat silently staring at the pen and pencil set on his desk.

"Well? Let's have it. What did you two work out?"

Gail cast him a sideways glance through her glasses, her demeanor one of serenity and composure. "Nothing. It seems as though I don't meet the congressman's qualifications."

"What do you mean?" The smile was gone from his face.

"I mean he wanted my life history before he'd hire me."

"And?"

"And nothing. I told him your recommendation ought to be enough."

"And?"

"And then I walked out before he could continue his line of third-degree questioning."

"Damn. I should have known." Sam's face reddened. "Can't I trust you two to have one simple little interview? I never saw two such opinionated people in my life. Neither one of you is willing to give the other the benefit of the doubt. Damn." He rolled his eyes toward the ceiling.

Gail leaned on the desk toward her boss. "Don't take it personally, Sam. This work relationship was just not meant to be."

"I don't buy that," he grumbled. "I just wish your father were here to talk some sense into you. Or if that didn't work—to take you over his knee." He glared at her. "'Cause that's sure what I'd like to do now."

Gail stood up. "Well, if anyone's going to be disciplined," she huffed, "I suggest you start with that bad boy congressman of yours. Now, if you'll excuse me, I've got work to do. Real work."

The telephone rang just as Sam was about to respond. He pointed a finger at Gail. "We'll get back to this later." Gail disappeared from view but couldn't help eavesdropping as she overheard Sam shouting on the phone. It was obviously the congressman on the other end and Sam was letting him know—in no uncertain terms how furious he was about what Gail had told him. Good, Gail thought, the man needed a good talking to.

GAIL KICKED off her loafers and stepped inside her tiny efficiency apartment. She threw her purse onto the sofa bed and padded in her stockinged feet toward the kitchen.

The mailbox had been empty today—not even an advertisement—so she sat down to read the *Washington Post* as she waited for her lamb chop to broil. She had stayed faithfully on her diet for three days now and felt smugly self-righteous as she carefully consumed the meager chop, an unadorned green salad and melba toast. Gail wasn't really overweight anymore—she could stand to lose a few pounds—but at just over five feet, she had to watch herself. She stretched her spartan supper through the paper as far as the society section, then brewed a cup of tea and sat back down to read about Washington's social scene. Before she had a chance to take a sip of tea, a familiar face jumped out at her. It was him—Brad Harrison, in all his tuxedoed glory. A picture taken at the reception the night before. As usual, a gorgeous woman stood by his side smiling up at him with unconcealed adoration.

Gail remembered her. She was a Washington groupie type who'd hovered around Brad as much as was possible, given her competition at the reception.

Gail studied the blonde in the picture and tried to avoid a comparison. She reminded herself that appearance was not important—not something to waste time on. Gail had decided all this some years before. A chubby child who became an overweight teenager, she had cushioned the pain of childish taunts by concentrating on her studies, deciding that it was the inner self that really mattered. Her decision had been constantly reaffirmed by comparisons she made between herself and the glamorous women she frequently met in Washington. She felt she couldn't hope to compete with these women as far as looks were concerned. This feeling of inadequacy was a catalyst in Gail's determination to shine intellectually and professionally, with scant attention given to feminine frills.

Gail had never attempted to master makeup. Her only concession to vanity was a dab of lipstick or rouge now and then. Tiny strands of hair, dishwater blond and baby fine, would work loose from her ponytail during the day making her look continually disheveled. Thick glasses obscured one of her best features—velvety dark brown eyes. People who looked closer saw the eyes, the soft porcelain skin, all the natural beauty. But Gail only saw imagined flaws and extra pounds, most of which had melted away years before.

Gail glanced again at the newspaper photograph, then sighed deeply as she rose from her chair and pulled open the freezer. What's the use? she asked herself. No matter how many diet dinners I suffer through, I'll never look that good. And it's obvious that Brad Harrison, most men for that matter, are only interested in the superficial aspects of women. Gail reached for the half gallon of pistachio almond fudge ice cream and grabbed a spoon from the cutlery drawer. She dug into the carton eagerly and savored a couple of mouthfuls but somehow the creamy sweet dessert didn't raise her flagging spirits.

What was wrong with her? she wondered. Why was she standing there brooding? Could it have anything to do with her exasperating encounter with Brad Harrison that morning? No. Of course not, she assured herself. She was probably just tired, that was all. A hot shower, then maybe a quick TV show and she'd be good as new.

Gail had just stepped out from the shower when a knock sounded at her door. Who in the world could that be? Probably her landlady, Mrs. Prince. She was the only pop-in caller Gail ever had. She grabbed her terry robe, then opened the chained door just a crack and peeked through. It couldn't be. Not him. Not Brad Harrison.

"May I come in?" He smiled.

"Just a minute," Gail stammered, attempting to sound calm. She slammed the door and leaned back against it. Should she let him in—after what happened this morning? Of course. He might be obnoxious, but he wasn't dangerous. She glanced around the room and then raced to scoot purse and shoes under the couch. Plate went in the sink. Coat and gloves were tossed onto the closet floor. Now where were her slippers? No time to search for them so she walked barefoot to the door, unlocked the chain and reluctantly opened it. Brad stepped inside.

"Wasn't sure you were going to let me in."

"It took some deliberation," she said, trying not to sound out of breath.

"I hope I didn't come at a bad time," Brad said, the glint in his eyes contradicting the message. His eyes moved down to her robe. Did he know she had nothing on underneath? She felt oddly vulnerable all of a sudden. He seemed to be stripping away the thick garment and almost caressing her bare skin with his gaze. Gail's face turned a soft pink under his scrutiny. Brad appeared to relish the moment. "I was on my way to a meeting and I thought I'd come by and apologize."

"It isn't necessary." Gail practically choked on her words, she was so overcome by the whole situation.

"Yes it is. I know now I did you a disservice questioning your ability. And Sam, too. Obviously he wouldn't recommend anyone he didn't have complete confidence in." His words sounded sincere but he was still watching her in that suggestive way.

Brad hadn't mentioned the other put-down, but then, she hadn't mentioned it to Sam, afraid he would laugh or worse, nag her again about her image.

Gail stood silently, her tongue frozen to the roof of her mouth. Where were all those clever comebacks she'd thought of earlier. She hated herself for her muteness right now and him even more for causing it.

"Well? Will you accept my apology?" Brad offered her his hand.

Gail stared at him, then at his hand as she shook it warily. It covered hers like a huge mitten and she felt even more self-conscious and miserable. She wanted to dash into the bathroom and lock the door.

Was it her imagination or was he laughing at her obvious distress? Was he trying to get revenge for the dressing down he'd taken from Sam this afternoon? She'd heard Sam on the phone, his voice raised almost to a shout. The senator from Arkansas had been furious, and rightfully so. After all, he'd offered him a member of his staff, someone he obviously respected and Brad had offended him by questioning her qualifications. It was a bad breach of political etiquette and Sam had made Brad eat crow.

Even though his words were contrite, his expression implied something else. He seemed to be getting some satisfaction from her dismay, her vulnerability as she stood there barefoot, nervously playing with the sash of her robe.

He cleared his throat. "Now that you've forgiven me, will you prove it by coming to work on my campaign?"

"You're putting me on."

"No," he protested. "I'm serious. Dead serious. And I won't take no for an answer."

"I'll have to discuss this with Sam. I told him I wouldn't be taking the job."

"No problem. I talked with him this afternoon and he gave me the green light. Along with a boot to the behind," he admitted. "Of course, Sam didn't know the half of it. Why did you cover for me? Most women I know would have relished recounting my rudeness."

"It would have been embarrassing."

"I suppose it would have . . . for both of us. But mostly for me. I appreciate your protecting me. That's one reason I want you to work for me."

"But—"

"No buts. I meant what I said. I won't take no for an answer."

"Well, I guess I can't fight you and Sam both. When do you want me to start?"

"Tomorrow afternoon," Brad answered. "Dave will get you oriented and next week the two of you will leave for New Orleans." He touched her shoulder. "Get your seat belt fastened. It's going to be a rough journey," he said, and vanished out the door.

Gail touched her shoulder—the same spot that Brad had patted. She shook her head. What was she letting herself in for?

GAIL LOOKED UP from the campaign profile she was reading and stole a quick glance at Dave. As Brad's advance man, he was compiling notes for the congressman's appearances over the next seven days, writing furiously on a yellow note pad. He and Gail were on an early-morning flight to New Orleans, Gail sipping juice and Dave draining a cup of coffee as they prepared themselves for the heavy schedule ahead. Dave looked up and gave her a quick smile. "Got a question?"

"No," she said. "It was nothing." She turned and stared out the window. Five days had quickly come and gone yet it seemed only hours ago that Brad had left her apartment. But the days had been intense, interesting and she'd already begun to feel like a member of the Harrison team.

That was Dave's doing. The man was a bonafide sweetheart—calm, gentle, patient. Everything his boss was not. Dave had made her feel welcome from the first minute they'd met, and he didn't seem to mind at all having to answer her endless questions.

Her only concern was making sure the relationship stayed on a business level. She was beginning to sense that Dave's interest in her might be other than professional. Gail wasn't attracted to him in that way. Too bad. He was such a nice guy. She could almost see him as a big brother. Funny how she classified the men she knew. She saw Sam as a father figure, Dave as a brother, and the few other men she knew were strictly in the "pal" category.

But Brad was another matter. He didn't fit into any category and that made Gail decidedly uncomfortable. She was beginning to find him appealing, maddeningly so. She berated herself as she thought of Brad and how his very presence brought butterflies to her stomach. How could she be attracted to a man as image conscious as Brad Harrison? Usually men like that, men who were smug and obviously aware of their looks, didn't interest her in the least. She must be losing her grip, she thought. She was hardly Brad's type. So why couldn't she stop thinking about him? She recalled the few times he'd joined her and Dave in their sessions in Washington. The moment he'd entered the office, her cool efficiency vanished. It took all her willpower to concentrate on the business at hand when her mind was playing tricks. Instead of thinking of campaign contributions and standings in voter polls, she found herself looking at him—thinking of what it would be like to be in his arms, having his lips touch hers. By the time the congressman excused himself, she'd have completely forgot about work. At times she wondered if he knew the effect he had on her and purposely tried to be disconcerting. She remembered his hand brushing against hers as they perused a campaign brochure...how her pulse had accelerated.

Enough of that, Gail, she instructed herself as she felt Dave watching her. "Is something wrong?" she asked, uncomfortable under his steady gaze.

"No. As a matter of fact, I was just thinking how lucky we are to have you working with us." He smiled. "To tell you the truth, I had some reservations about your being able to hack it."

"Oh? And now?"

"And now," he answered, "I'm wondering if the rest of us will be able to keep up with you."

"Thanks, Dave." She touched his hand lightly. "I just hope our boss will feel the same way."

"Brad? He'll be as crazy about you as I am in no time." His pale gray eyes shone. Gail turned away embarrassed.

"About this profile," she said, changing the subject as she flipped through some pages. Soon they were back on a topic she felt secure about as the plane soared southward.

They arrived on time, and it wasn't long before Gail and Dave were settled in adjoining rooms, at a small old hotel in the French Quarter of New Orleans. After they'd had a chance to freshen up, they walked over to the Harrison campaign headquarters, which was only a few blocks away on Canal Street. The narrow storefront was overshadowed by a huge sign with the name Harrison painted in bold red letters on a blue background with white stars, and a large picture of Brad hung below, covering the window.

It was an effective political photo. Brad's slight, concerned-looking squint and his friendly half smile would surely help him draw some votes.

"Not too fancy, is it?" she asked Dave as they stood on the sidewalk in front eyeing the premises.

"Well, Gail, you and I both know that campaigns are not won or lost by fancy campaign headquarters. If they were, Merton Ramsey would have already imported Buckingham Palace."

"Or the Taj Mahal," Gail laughed as they entered the front door.

Gail and Dave had scheduled a strategy session for one o'clock and the workers were there when they entered. Introductions were made, then Dave led the session, laying out their perceptions of the current campaign problems. By the time the meeting ended three hours later, Gail was acutely aware of the battle that loomed ahead.

"Whew!" she said to Dave. "I've really got my work cut out for me here."

Dave nodded solemnly. "But right now it's time for a break," he said looking at his watch. "Why don't we take our minds off the campaign for a couple of hours with a quick tour of the French Quarter?"

"Sounds good," Gail agreed. "Right now I feel too overwhelmed to work anyway."

"Have you been to New Orleans before?" Dave inquired. They were walking down Royal Street headed toward Jackson Square.

"No, this is my first visit."

"That's great. One of my favorite roles is tour guide. To your right, mademoiselle, is the famed Casa Hove, where fragrances have been created for over a century. Then, if you'll just look back as we turn this corner, there's the famous Preservation Hall, home of some jazz greats."

"Impressive. You sound like a native," Gail laughed merrily.

"I am—well almost. I grew up in Gretna, just down the river apiece. As a younger man I spent many an hour here."

"How did you become involved in politics, and with Brad?" she asked as they continued walking.

"Brad and my older brother met in the service. They were assigned to the same carrier and one day discovered they were both Louisiana boys, almost neighbors, in fact. They became close friends and that's how I met Brad." He reached up and brushed the hair off his forehead. "My brother got me a job working for Brad during summers off from high school and we hit it off real well. Right after I graduated from L.S.U., he was running for Congress the first time. He didn't have anyone in particular lined up to be campaign manager and I didn't have any particular job lined up. So, I just sort of wheedled my way into the campaign. I guess he was satisfied because I've been around ever since."

"Sounds like you're rather fond of him."

"I like him and respect him. Frankly, there aren't too many men around I can say that about."

"Not even your brother?"

"Unfortunately, no longer. Flying jets off carriers is a dangerous job. He was killed in a crash."

"I'm sorry," Gail said.

They turned the corner onto Chartres Street. "Enough of that, I feel like playing tour guide again. Across the street, my dear, is the famed Jackson Square, with old Andy himself astride his trusty mount." He pointed to the statue of Andrew Jackson, which was playing host to a gathering of pigeons.

Dave smiled. "Old Hickory would have shot and roasted those damned birds if he'd seen them on his likeness." Gail chuckled.

Dave led her over to a flight of steps. "Here you will find the mighty Mississippi River." They gazed out from their platform view at the expanse of water. In size alone the river was an impressive sight, but it looked even more dazzling with an array of commercial ships and several showboats traveling its course.

"Tour's over," Dave said quickly. "Now let's have a drink." He clasped Gail's hand as they descended the steps and crossed the street heading back toward the square.

They walked a couple of blocks, then entered an old bar and ordered beer.

"I have to say one thing, Mr. McElroy," Gail smiled, "You're a most efficient guide. No words wasted."

Dave responded in good humor. "Well, that's the best I can come up with for the price of a beer. To get the deluxe tour, you have to buy me dinner."

Gail sidestepped his suggestion about dinner, light-heartedly commenting, "I thought you invited me for this drink—now you tell me I'm paying! What gall," she said sarcastically, giving an exaggerated sigh.

"Gail," Dave placed his hand over hers on the table. The playfulness in his eyes was gone.

Self-consciously she pulled her hand away and rested it in her lap. Then after a few moments of awkward silence, Gail found her voice. "Dave, I really have to be getting back. I've some phone calls to make. Thanks for the walk." She reached into her purse for some money.

"Don't be silly, Gail," Dave protested. "I'm paying."

"Oh, no," said Gail adamantly, "for two beers it was still a cheap tour."

"Well, okay," he relented. "But next time it's on me."

"That's a deal," she said. They left the bar and slowly made their way back to the office.

The next morning Gail drove with Dave to the front gates of a glove factory. This was the first stop on the Louisiana campaign trail, which Gail had mapped out for Brad's brief visit to the state. It was 5:55 a.m. and Brad was due to begin shaking hands in five minutes. She and Dave parked the car and took their places near the gate, placing boxes of cards and buttons nearby to pass out to workers going in.

"He's not here yet," she said to Dave. She was both pleased and troubled. She had devilishly planned this early morning event in order to intimidate the night owl candidate. But what if he didn't make it at all?

But her concern faded as a cab drove up and deposited Brad right at the gate. He was wearing a navy raincoat and carried a big red-and-white umbrella. He glared at Gail, and said half kiddingly, "The next time you schedule me for six a.m., you're fired." Just then rain began falling. "Did you arrange this weather, too?" he grumbled, in obvious bad humor. Gail had to stifle a laugh. The rain was falling harder, beginning to drench her hair and suit and saturate her shoes, but she decided it was worth it to witness Brad's discomfort.

Brad opened his umbrella. "Here," he said shoving it into her hand. "Make yourself useful." Gail looked incredulous as she realized he intended for her to hold the opened umbrella over his head. She had to stand on tiptoe and stretch her arm its full length to accommodate the difference in their heights. "Thank you." He smiled, arching one eyebrow.

"Anything for the candidate," Gail replied waspishly.

The employees began to file in through the gates as Brad started working the crowd. Standing beside him with umbrella and arm extended, Gail was able to watch Brad in action. She had to admit his performance was first-rate. Most of the workers at this plant were men and Brad was able to communicate with them naturally—he seemed to know just what to say. He talked with them as equals, sharing their concerns and explaining how he might be able to help.

As Brad chatted, Dave passed out campaign literature and Gail continued holding the umbrella. The three of them stood in place for two hours until the last day worker was inside the plant. They had also managed to greet the night workers ending their shift. Gail's arm ached and she was more irritated than ever at Brad. He flashed her another smile as he took the umbrella, closed it and motioned toward Dave's rental car. "And what's next on our agenda, Ms Meredith?"

A group of local campaign volunteers was in the small headquarters when they arrived about an hour later. Brad was scheduled to make a brief presentation to them—a pep talk of sorts to keep their spirits at high level.

A hush spread over them as the threesome entered, then polite applause. Brad smiled, said a few personal hellos, then went over to a desk and sat casually on the corner. He unbuttoned his blazer and smiled.

"Friends," he began. "I want to take this opportunity to tell you how much I appreciate your help." The staffers smiled expectantly as Brad continued. He explained that this was an uphill battle, one he intended to pursue until the end—until the general election and victory in November.

"This fight is a crucial one for the people of Louisiana and we can't afford to leave our children a wasteland."

Brad narrowed his eyes. "So we must all double our efforts to win this battle against the likes of a Merton Ramsey who would sell this state to the highest bidder if we let him get away with it." He slammed his fist into his hand. "I, for one, will not let that happen." He paused. "And I hope you'll be with me all the way—all the way to victory!"

The group applauded enthusiastically. Brad smiled. "Now let's have a cup of that good coffee before I get back out there on the campaign trail."

Gail watched him as he mingled with the volunteers. Well, she thought, he was good at being a politician. He was definitely in the right business.

Dave gave Brad an eye signal that it was time to push on, and Brad politely eased himself away from the group surrounding him. "Gotta go," he said. "The slave drivers who manage my campaign are telling me it's time to move along. Keep up the good work, while I'm in Washington." He gave a wave and a broad grin and walked out quickly with Gail and Dave following.

Just as they reached the curb, a shiny black Ferrari screeched to a halt in front of them. Brad gave a show of recognition then pulled open the door. "See you tomorrow," he said to Dave and Gail as he climbed into the low-slung car. Gail recognized Judith DeWitt and suddenly felt strangely depressed.

"What's she doing here?" she asked Dave.

"New Orleans is Judith's home."

"But I thought Brad was set up to meet with some financial backers this afternoon." She tried not to sound upset.

"Well Judith has funnelled plenty of money into his campaign. So I guess that makes her a backer. Besides, they're old pals."

"I'll just bet they are," Gail grumbled.

"Cynicism isn't becoming to pretty women." Dave took her arm and linked it through his. "Now how about some lunch?"

CHAPTER THREE

THE NEXT MORNING was hectic. They visited a nursing home in a small town outside the city where Brad made a speech, then the candidate participated in a ribbon cutting ceremony for a new bridge.

The three then retreated to a small restaurant for lunch where they huddled in a back booth for privacy. "Well, Gail," Brad pushed his plate away, "do you think you can handle things while Dave's back in Washington with me next week?"

Gail was offended. Dave was a top-notch campaign organizer, but he didn't have a monopoly on ability. Did this chauvinist think she couldn't function without a male looking over her shoulder? Fortunately Dave came to her rescue just as she opened her mouth to give Brad an earful.

"Brad, I think Gail can manage without me—maybe even without you. In case you haven't noticed, she's one hell of a politician." Dave's voice had an edge to it—a cutting edge.

Brad smiled at Gail as he responded to Dave. "I'm sure she is one hell of a politician as you say, Dave. I just thought she might need some help, being new to the state and all."

Gail didn't believe one word he said, but she couldn't think of an appropriate response. She continued eating her lunch solemnly while Brad and Dave evaluated the campaign to date. Despite the enthusiastic response they had received, Brad was still dragging in the polls, and that was distressing to Gail; she hadn't been anxious to get on this campaign bandwagon, but now that she was, she hoped to see it be a winning one. Maybe the polls would show a shift in a week or two. Maybe it was just too early to know yet.

They dropped Brad off downtown; he offered no explanation as to where he was going. Probably to see Judith DeWitt again, Gail thought. Who could blame him? Judith was a beautiful, desirable woman. And—Gail thought wishfully—probably has the I.Q. of a kumquat.

Brad didn't reappear until late Sunday. He'd instructed them not to schedule any appearances for the weekend. Gail was annoyed that he'd simply decided to vanish into thin air, that he was wasting valuable time on personal matters. At the least he might have telephoned to check on the campaign. But there had been no word from him since he'd disappeared three days before.

Gail was cloistered in a back room of the headquarters rewriting some campaign brochures. The office was empty. Few volunteers, no matter how enthusiastic, spent their Sunday afternoons working. She had just highlighted several sentences on a brochure when she heard a floorboard creak. Startled, she looked up, realizing she wasn't alone. It was Brad. "Well, if it isn't little Miss Busy Bee," he drawled lazily, leaning against the door frame.

Gail's nerves, now unsteady, bristled at his mocking tone. His unexpected presence made her uncomfortable, even more so as he came to glance over her shoulder. She realized that, for the first time since he'd hired her, she and Brad were totally alone. There was no receptionist seated outside the door to protect her. She stood up and glared at him, but the intended impact was lessened by the fact that her eyes were at the level of his tie. She felt flushed. "Get a lot of work done this weekend?'' she finally managed defensively.

"Personal work I'm afraid," Brad answered, his face registering surprise at her question.

I'll just bet, Gail wanted to say. She recovered her composure quickly enough to smile and say, "Well, great. Now maybe you'll have some time to look after your congressional business when you get back to Washington."

Brad's eyes flashed angrily. "I don't know what you're implying by that," he snapped, "but you listen, and listen good." His voice was low, his irritation barely concealed. "It's about time we get something straight." He grabbed her arms almost lifting her from the floor. "I know you don't cherish the idea of working on the lowly campaign of some Louisiana congressman. I'm sure you think you're more suited for presidential duty. But let's just get it clear—it's sufferance on both our parts. I need the support of Sam and his cronies on this campaign. You came with the deal—I agreed to go along with it for fear of upsetting Sam. But don't push your luck too far! Understand?" His hands gripped her arms tighter, his face only inches from hers.

Gail opened her mouth to protest, then looked up into his stormy eyes. They had darkened to a royal blue. Suddenly, without warning, Gail's thoughts were interrupted by Brad's lips on hers. His kiss was forceful, almost punishing. She tried to push away but her arms were no match for his restraining grasp. And, if the truth were known, her resistance was beginning to wane as the kiss continued. Finally, Brad released her and stepped back, an odd expression on his face.

Why was he looking at her that way? Why had he been so mad at her? Politicians usually had skins like rhinoceros hides. They had to to survive. Why had he lost his cool? Gail didn't know the answer. "I didn't mean to upset you," she stammered. What am I saying? she thought. I'm the one who's upset. The man just kissed me.

Brad's composure seemed to be returning as he responded. "Then you need to keep in mind that I don't like having my professionalism questioned—by anyone." That didn't sound like a reason for kissing someone, she thought. But, she reminded herself, it wasn't really a kiss, more an angry reaction. Brad was looking at her, that unreadable look making her even more uncomfortable. She was relieved when he finally spoke. "Look, can we forget that all this ever happened and try to go on about our business?"

Gail nodded. But she knew it would be hard to erase this whole scene from her mind.

GAIL RETURNED to Washington for a briefing with Dave and two aides a week later.

"Now this is the way I look at it." Dave was standing in front of an easel, pointing to some handwritten notes scribbled there. Gail was seated at a small table, Tom and Evelyn, two other campaign assistants beside her. They each had a tablet, a pen and an empty coffee cup in front of them. "Brad feels that he's not getting through to the voters with his message." Dave flipped through to a second page. "These are the points that Brad wants emphasized in the next few weeks. Now, who has any ideas?"

The three of them sat quietly facing Dave. "Well? Any suggestions on putting it all together?" Dave looked at each of them.

"Why don't you let me work something up?" Gail volunteered. "I think I can come up with one or two good suggestions, Dave. I don't have to be back in Louisiana for a couple of days and that'll give me time to do some quick research."

"Okay, then, go to it." Dave did not sound enthusiastic. "But remember—Brad is a tough guy to please."

"I'll keep that in mind every step of the way." Her tone was sarcastic. As if anyone needed to remind her about Brad.

It took Gail four days, instead of the two she had planned, to do the research and write the report for Brad. But it was a labor of love for Gail who had made a serious commitment to environmental protection. It had been one of her father's interests during his legislative career. As she studied the subject, she was surprised to see the name Brad Harrison mentioned two or three times as a lawmaker with environmental interests. But for all she knew, that could be part of a public relations profile.

She turned the report in to Dave Saturday afternoon, and not a moment too soon; she had chores to complete and errands to run before flying back to New Orleans on Sunday.

By seven, Gail was putting the finishing touches on a large chef salad when she heard a knock at the door. "That's funny," she said aloud, wondering who it could be. Few people knew that she was back in Washington. She walked to the door and opened it cautiously, the chain lock still intact. Not again. She shuddered. It was Brad Harrison.

She closed the door and slid off the chain, the reopened it. "Hello," she said almost shyly, aware she was dressed, fresh from a shower, in an old flowered muumuu. Her wet hair was wrapped in a white terry towel and her feet were bare.

Brad smiled as he eyed her appearance. "I seem to be making a habit of catching you at the wrong time. May I come in for a minute?"

"Oh, of course." Gail was apologetic. "Come in. I'm sorry to be so ungracious. I—uh...just wasn't expecting company." She stepped back to let him enter.

"Please, Gail, don't apologize." He took in the apartment as he spoke, making Gail miserably aware of the mess—her suitcase in the middle of the floor, half-packed; salad fixings all over the kitchen; and wet lingerie visible through the open bathroom door.

"But," he continued, "I just wanted to tell you something before you left tomorrow."

"Oh?" she asked.

"Yes," he answered. "I finished reading your paper late this afternoon and I had to tell you in person what a fine job you did on it."

"Oh?" she repeated, her brown eyes shining through her glasses. Was he offering an olive branch?

"It's terrific. As a matter of fact, I'm not sure I could have done any better." He looked at her and smiled broadly, causing her knees to feel like gelatin. "Gail, you are a very capable person." He patted her on the arm. "Well, gotta go. Keep up the good work," he said and was out of the apartment before Gail could say goodbye.

Gail stood transfixed for a few seconds, Brad's words replaying in her head. At first she had reacted with pleasure to the compliment. But the more she thought about it, the more depressed she became. A very capable person, he'd called her. Why did she suddenly feel neutered, she wondered, staring in the small mirror over the couch. Why had she let this irritating man come into her private life and upset her? Sighing dejectedly she padded back into the kitchen. "This campaign can't be over soon enough to suit me,'' she said aloud. *I'm tired of simpering over an arrogant boss who treats me like the family dog. A pat on the head one minute and a foot in the flank the next. My life was fine before and it'll be fine again just as soon as Brad Harrison is out of it.*

Gail left for New Orleans on a late-morning flight. For some reason she felt a little empty seeing the Washington landscape disappear from view. Why? Was she still obsessed with the night before? Nonsense, she told herself. She was glad to be putting a thousand miles between herself and Brad. Maybe now she would be free of his intimidating put-downs. Why did she make it so easy for him to get under her skin?

She had suffered now through two impromptu visits by a man who looked as if he'd just stepped from a Brooks Brothers ad. He had been wearing a navy business suit the night before and the dark color contrasted effectively with his sun-bleached hair. Likely he had just showered and shaved, because his skin shone and Gail had noticed the fresh smell of cologne.

Why had she been dressed in a faded flowered muumuu of all things? The answer was obvious. She had worn that old thing for years and she liked it. There was nothing more comfortable. Gail resolved to turn that muumuu into a dust rag before the week was out and to find something more attractive to wear around the house. She was certainly not going to be caught like that again. But by the end of the week, enmeshed in work, she'd forgotten her vow and was back in her small room in New Orleans, wearing her muumuu, eating take-out Chinese food.

Brad flew into town the following weekend to attend a testimonial dinner for a former mayor of New Orleans. With Dave tied up in Washington, Gail was in charge of chauffeuring the candidate around. She drove him to the dinner, returned him to his hotel, and picked him up the next morning for a breakfast meeting with a labor group.

"Where to now?" Gail asked as they got back into the car after breakfast. There were no scheduled activities. "Want to work a shopping center before lunch?"

Brad shook his head. "No, I really need to take care of some personal matters."

Here it comes, Gail thought, the escape again—probably to the DeWitt mansion.

"If it's okay with you," Brad said, "I'll just drop you off and the take the car to— On second thought, why don't you come with me?"

Gail looked over at him. "Come with you?"

"Sure. Unless you're too busy."

"No, no I'm not busy—but where are we going?"

Brad came around the car to the driver's side. "To see a very special lady." Gail slid over wondering just who this special lady could be. Brad got behind the wheel. They were soon on the freeway heading in the direction of Baton Rouge.

About fifteen miles out of the city, Brad turned off the main highway onto a small winding road. In a few minutes they came up to an arched sign, which read Greenbriar Plantation.

Brad turned onto the tree-lined gravel road and drove toward a beautiful old antebellum house—a Greek Revival style mansion with a squared central section flanked by two rectangular wings. Two-story white columns sat at intervals across the entire front and soared to the roof. The whiteness of the house was contrasted by black shutters, which ran the length of floor-to-ceiling windows. Blooming magnolia trees, plants and colorful flowers were everywhere. It was a pretty sight—the owner certainly couldn't be lacking in wealth, Gail thought.

"Is this 'special lady' here?" asked Gail as Brad helped her from the car.

"She sure is," Brad answered, "and she'll be tickled pink that I brought a guest."

Before they could get up the steps, the front door swung open and an elderly woman came out to greet them. She had gray-blue hair and was slightly stooped. She looked about seventy, but she was youthfully dressed in slacks, an overblouse, clanky gold chains and espadrilles.

"Bradley, I thought I heard you drive up." She looked at Gail. "And you brought company."

"That's right, you crazy old woman. This is my state campaign manager, Gail Meredith. Now you be nice to her, and no cussing or spitting while we're here."

The woman laughed. "Bradley Harrison! What would you have people think of me." She looked down at Gail. "Hello, dear. I'm Brad's Aunt Sussy." She shook Gail's hand. "I'm very glad to have you here."

"Thank you," answered Gail. "Brad told me that he had someone very special for me to meet."

"Don't tell her that," said Brad as he came bounding up the steps. "You'll give her a big head, and this old woman's hard enough to get along with as it is." He put an arm around his aunt and gave her a squeeze.

Gail could see the obvious affection between the two. She wondered if Brad's aunt knew what kind of reputation her nephew had with women. Or, she mused, examining Aunt Sussy again, if she cared.

Brad and Gail followed the woman into the house. They made their way through a large hallway to the parlor, a high-ceilinged reception room with gleaming parquet floors. Bookshelves lined one wall and small antique tables and chairs had been placed in little groupings throughout the elegant room. The small sofa on the far wall had been covered in a pretty floral printed fabric, adding a splash of color to the otherwise dark decor.

"Calvin," said Aunt Sussy, to one butler who had followed them into the parlor. "We'd like some lemonade in here."

"Yes, ma'am," he answered and quickly left, and returned carrying a tray with a crystal pitcher filled with ice, sliced lemon, what looked to be freshly squeezed lemonade and three crystal goblets. Aunt Sussy filled the glasses and passed them each one. Gail had forgotten how good cold lemonade could taste. She wondered whether it was the luxurious surroundings or being treated so kindly, that suddenly made her feel so special.

They chatted for over an hour as they sipped the tart juice. Aunt Sussy had demanded that Brad and Gail give her the latest figures on Brad's standings in the polls. Gail was amazed Aunt Sussy knew as much as she did. She had obviously been following the campaign every step of the way. Gail took an instinctive liking to the older woman and admired her quick wit. "Congressman," Gail said, "you should have hired your aunt as campaign manager. She's as smart as they come."

Brad gave an exaggerated snort. "Hire that crazy old lady! Why she'd have me in hot water the first week." He winked at Gail. "When people discovered we were related, they'd rush like wildfire to support my opponents. No, this old lady has to stay out here in the country, away from cameras and newspapers."

Gail looked at Aunt Sussy to see how she was taking Brad's ribbing. Without a doubt, she was loving it. "You young fool," she shouted back at Brad in jest. "I'm too busy to waste my time politicking for the likes of you. Besides—" she looked straight at Gail "—it looks to me like you're in pretty good hands as it is."

Brad made no response and Gail could feel her cheeks redden at the compliment. She took a final sip of lemonade as Brad announced they had to go.

The three exchanged goodbyes and Brad and Gail made their way toward the car. "Oh, Gail," called Aunt Sussy, "there's one more thing." Gail went back to the door and Brad's aunt spoke softly into her ear. "Take care of my nephew. He needs a nice woman in his life."

Gail was surprised. She wanted to tell her that Brad would hardly be interested in her—and if there was anything in this world he needed, it certainly wasn't another woman in his life. But his aunt seemed so sincere; she even gave her a brief hug. So Gail made no comment. She simply trotted back down the stairs, shaking her head in wonderment.

They drove back to New Orleans in silence. Gail initiated a couple of efforts at conversation but Brad was uncooperative, giving only token "uh-huhs" to her comments. This Jekyll and Hyde routine of Brad's was disturbing. One minute he was totally charming, almost bubbly, with his aunt, and the next, alone with Gail, he had turned into a clam. Obviously the garrulous routine at the plantation was just an act, another performance by the political animal seated next to her. Either that, Gail reasoned, or Brad couldn't stand being with her. Not even enough to be sociable, to make polite conversation. But if that were true, why had he taken her to Greenbriar in the first place? Was he upset she had lingered with his aunt during their goodbyes? Who could tell with him? She would be relieved to have him back in Washington.

"HAVE YOU SEEN the papers?" It was Dave calling from Washington. Gail looked over at the bedside clock. Five-thirty? She sat upright.

"What's happened?" She was awake enough now to be concerned.

"Well, Brad's bought himself a pack of trouble for sure. The press is having a field day here. I haven't talked to Brad yet so I don't have any details. But it seems as though he and his dinner date, a secretary on Capitol Hill, ran into her former boyfriend at a restaurant in Georgetown. The boyfriend didn't like Brad's looks and did a little plastic surgery—with his fists. And it's all over the papers, not to mention TV."

"Oh, no," Gail moaned.

"Oh, yes," Dave answered, agitation in his voice. "Anyway, Gail, check out the media coverage down there and get back to me as soon as possible. We've got to figure out how much damage has been done." He hung up.

Gail got up and dressed quickly, throwing on a turtleneck and denim skirt and headed out in search of a newsstand.

She arrived at the campaign headquarters laden down with local papers from around the state. "Stop what you're doing and help me go through these," she said to a secretary who was hunched over a typewriter.

As the television blared the morning news in the background, the two went quickly through the papers Gail had accumulated. The same picture was in every one. Brad and his date leaving the restaurant, he with his lapel ripped off and one eye battered shut. Gail called Dave back. "It's not a good picture of Brad," she said sardonically. "One eye seems to be squinting."

"Don't be cute," Dave answered. "Just tell me how bad it is down there."

"Well," she said, "all the morning newspapers picked up the story and ran the picture. But the television coverage appears to be limited to the New Orleans area. At least

I haven't heard from any of the parish chairmen yet. I'll put through some calls later on this morning."

"Yeah, I'd like to hear their reactions and find out if everyone from Grand Isle to Vivian and all points in between has seen this debacle on TV. Listen, Gail, we'll be in touch. 'Bye now."

It was the next morning before Dave got back to her. "Thank goodness," she said, "I've just about had it giving 'no comment' statements to the press."

"Well, don't stop yet," instructed Dave. "Just keep your lips sealed in a fixed smile until you're out of town. I want you to fly up as soon as possible for a briefing. Be prepared to stay for two or three days," he added.

By ten the next morning, Gail, Dave, Brad, Tom and Evelyn had all come together in Brad's office. At Brad's invitation, Sam had joined them. It was a subdued group, sitting mutely as Dave stood before them, a report in his hand, which they were all eyeing warily. "What all this says in so many words," he said waving the pages, "is that Brad has plummeted in the polls. That pugilistic exercise at Mario's Restaurant the other night seems to have hurt more than his looks." Dave looked at Brad and smiled faintly.

Brad banged his fist on the table. "Somebody is making a lot out of nothing! What happened to the issues in this race?"

Sam squeezed Brad's arm. "Brad, you know the games the press and politicians play. They're not going to talk issues when there's something else to spotlight. And what makes for better conversation than a romantic triangle? No, Brad, you stepped right into this one. Of course, there's a possibility this was a set-up. There was a lot of press around. And I suggest you people check into it." Sam looked around the room, "but please, do it discreetly! We don't need any more waves. Right now Merton Ramsey's got Brad just where he wants him—looking like some playboy politician. Meanwhile, Ramsey just sits back acting the mature family man, indignant that the likes of Brad Harrison would have the nerve to run against him.''

Sam reached for the newspapers he had brought with him. ''Look at this picture of Merton in the *Times Picayune* and his quote. 'I'm shocked','' Sam read, '''to discover the caliber of candidates the other party is running in this primary. They sound like a bunch of degenerates—a defrocked preacher, a tax evader, and now this playboy who spends the taxpayers' money sparring in nightclubs.''' Sam snorted as he held up the picture and read the next line. The picture showed Merton with his arm around a small boy in a baseball uniform. '''What the good people of Louisiana need as their senator is a dependable family man—one who cares about the people he is representing—not an irresponsible boy still playing games.'''

''Boy?'' Brad shot Sam a look of disgust. ''At thirty-six, I must be the world's oldest 'boy.''' He rose from his chair. ''That damn Ramsey—that no-good hypocrite.''

''Settle down, Brad,'' said Sam. ''Your getting upset is not going to help anyone. What you're going to have to do is cool it.'' Sam wiped off the beads of perspiration forming on his forehead. ''Though I'm not sure that cooling it will help at this point—what you really need is to dispel this playboy image.''

''What do you suggest I do?'' Brad asked cynically. ''Perhaps we could have my dear mother separate herself from husband number five—or is it six?—and return home to help with the campaigning. That would present a lovely picture for the voters, wouldn't it?'' he snarled. He loosened his tie and slumped back into his chair.

Sam came around and gave him a paternal pat on the shoulders. "Come on, Brad, calm down. For now, let's just try to forget old wounds and see if we can come up with a solution."

Gail rose, coffee cup in hand. "Obviously, there's only one solution," she said flippantly. She pointed to a picture of Merton Ramsey and his family. "The congressman simply has to get a wife." She cast a sidelong glance at Brad. "He could probably arrange it with a couple of phone calls and we could be making the announcement within hours. Anyone else want coffee?" she asked casually, heading toward the hall to pour some for herself when no one responded.

Once she was alone, she took a deep breath. She knew her annoyance had shown, but those pictures with that— that female draped around Brad had made her furious. How could he be so stupid as to let himself get in a situation like that? To blow all the hard work they'd done.

It was proof again of how right she'd been not to want this assignment. Every time she got excited about the campaign, began to raise her opinion of Brad as a viable candidate, he'd do something to diminish her optimism. He never failed to disappoint her. Now what? More of the same, she guessed. She'd go back in and give it another try.

Gail opened the door, surprised to see the group sitting frozen in place. It was clear nothing had happened during her absence. She sat down quietly and sipped her coffee. The strong brew was as terrible as ever.

Sam shattered the calm and shocked everyone by banging his fist on the table. "By damn, if Gail hasn't hit the nail right on the head. Brad needs to get married!"

Everyone stared incredulously at Sam.

"This is no time for jokes," Brad grumbled.

"I'm not kidding," Sam responded. "That's the one thing that would take the heat off from Merton and Brad's other worthy opponents." He looked at Brad. "You need a wife, Congressman, and you need one now!"

"That's a hell of a note—my marital status is more important than my platform."

"But, Brad," said Dave. "Sam has a point. If you were married, Merton couldn't dwell on your image. He'd have to talk issues."

Brad stood, agitation showing on his face. He moved toward the door. "I don't have time for such foolishness. Sam, I appreciate your coming over to meet with us, but I've got to go to that committee hearing now. When the rest of you come up with some serious suggestions, let me know." He slammed the door behind him.

"Well, so much for Brad's imminent marriage," said Tom staring at Brad's empty chair.

No one spoke. Then Dave looked at his watch. "Listen, it's close to lunchtime. Let's take a break." Gail and Sam remained seated as the others left the room.

"Life was a lot calmer in the Dirksen Building," she muttered. Gail looked to Sam for a response but he didn't reply. He remained silent, watching her with a strange expression on his face.

"What's the matter, Sam?"

"Nothing," he answered absently. "I'd better go now, Gail. I'll talk to you later."

Gail was surprised to hear from Sam again that afternoon. "I want you over at my house for cocktails," he ordered. "Five-thirty okay?"

"Since when do you have cocktail parties, Sam?" Gail asked.

"Since now," he replied. "I'll see you at five-thirty," he said, and hung up.

When she arrived at Sam's town house, Gail was surprised to find Brad there, highball glass in hand, seated in a lounge chair. He looked just as surprised to see her and shrugged his shoulders obviously wondering why Sam had summoned them there. Clearly both had realized Sam had more in mind than cocktails.

Gail gave him a weak smile and followed Sam into the kitchen. Something was wrong. "What's going on, Sam?" She had a no-nonsense look in her eyes.

"What can I get you to drink?" Sam said, sidestepping her question.

"A Tom Collins, I guess. Now, tell me what you're up to?"

Sam sliced a lemon and squeezed it into her glass. "All in good time, my dear—first your drink." He stirred in a spoonful of sugar, then added the soda.

Gail sighed in exasperation. She knew there was no hurrying Sam. He was the most obstinate man alive and he wouldn't explain until he was good and ready.

They joined Brad in the living room, Sam taking the other lounge chair and Gail the sofa. Brad and Gail sat silently waiting for Sam to speak his mind.

Sam smiled coyly at each of them. "I'm not sure how to begin—so I'll just jump right in. I think you two ought to get married."

No one said a word. Gail was sure she could hear her own heart beat. Brad and Gail turned and stared at each other then at Sam. Their expressions clearly posed the same question. Is this man serious?

"Okay, okay," said Sam. "I can see what you're thinking. You're both wondering if I've lost all my marbles."

"That's about it," Brad said caustically.

"Well, let me assure you that I'm in control of all my faculties." Sam drained his shot glass of whiskey, then sat upright. He eyed them over the top of his glasses.

"Brad, whether you know it or not, you need a wife in the worst way. Merton and your other opponents are making mincemeat out of you. That little display of fisticuffs was just the icing on their cakes." He pulled a pipe from the ashtray on the table next to his chair and lit it.

"There's no way you can rally now. You're on the ropes and the beating will continue right up to election day unless..." Sam blew some smoke into the air. "Unless you can disarm them—with Gail."

"No offense, Gail," said Brad giving her a quick glance as he turned to Sam. "But, Sam, that is the dumbest thing you've ever said. Besides, what's in it for Gail?"

Sam smiled. "I don't think it's dumb at all. But, we'll get to Gail in a minute. Let's concentrate on you first, Brad. There are two things for you to keep in mind. One— you need a wife. A wife like Gail to eliminate your playboy image and force your opponents to stick to the issues. Two—with a wife like Gail, you can win, Brad—*win*, and then you can pursue your new ideas in the Senate."

Brad rose from his chair. "I need another drink." He disappeared into the kitchen.

"And now, Gail." Sam looked at her. "What can I say to convince you?"

When Gail didn't respond, he began to answer his own question. "I guess I could appeal to your nobler instincts—tell you that Brad needs you desperately, that without you he can't win. Or perhaps I could remind you that a senator like Brad could ensure that environmental protection gets the attention it deserves in the Congress. Or maybe I could even suggest that this marriage could give you your own political base. Other wives of politicians have gone on to have careers in politics.''

Gail sipped her drink as Sam talked, absorbing the words. ''Well, there might be some merit in what you say,'' she agreed. ''But I can't seem to get past the point where Brad needs a wife like me. In other words, you're saying he needs someone plain enough to erase his playboy image. Did it ever occur to you that he might have a more attractive bride in mind?''

''Now, Gail, cut that out. Have I ever—and I repeat ever—insinuated that I think you're plain? Why, you're one of the prettiest women I've ever known. You're also warm, bright and witty.'' His eyes shone through his thick glasses as he stared at her.

''I wasn't fishing for compliments, Sam,'' Gail responded shyly. ''But as I said, Brad needs to choose his own wife.''

Brad had been standing at the door long enough to hear Gail's last comment. He walked across the room and slumped back into his chair.

''Well, Congressman,'' Sam said, ''you heard the lady. Do you have another potential bride dangling?''

''No,'' Brad snarled. ''Marriage has not been one of my priorities, you know. Experience hasn't given me much respect for the institution.'' He stared down at the liquid in his glass.

''Besides, even if I did have someone, I still think marriage is a hell of a bad solution for a lagging campaign. God knows I've willingly made concessions for the sake of the race—eaten pounds of rubbery chicken, kissed babies with runny noses, made speeches in rainstorms. But this— Sam, don't you think marriage is a bit far-fetched, a rather extreme campaign gambit?''

"Do you have any other ideas for turning this debacle around?" Sam challenged.

"No, dammit," Brad took a swallow of his drink. "It looks like I'm pretty well painted into a corner." He slumped lower in the chair and continued to nurse his drink. Traffic from outside intruded on the silence as Gail rose and walked over to the window, staring sightlessly out at the street. Sam must be losing his grip. But so must she, not to have walked out the minute he mentioned this. How could she get married to save a political campaign, and of all people to that lady-killer across the room? She felt like a frightened rabbit trying to stay out of his snare. So why hadn't she just said "No!" and been done with it? Why hadn't Brad? Why did he appear to be pondering Sam's words? Surely the idea couldn't appeal to him any more than it did to her. Then it struck her. Not marriage, but the idea of salvaging his campaign was appealing—very appealing. Even if he had to sacrifice his bachelorhood. In shock, she turned around to hear Brad saying, "If everyone's so damned insistent on this marriage deal, I suppose I ought to consider it."

"To Gail?" Sam prompted.

"Well there's no big romance in my life. I guess Gail's as good as anyone."

Gail almost bit her tongue off avoiding a caustic response. As good as anyone? They sounded as though they were selecting campaign buttons. Brad's patronizing attitude particularly infuriated her. As good as anyone, indeed. The words screamed through her mind. Gail gripped the glass she was holding so tightly her knuckles turned white. She wanted to throw the glass straight at Brad. Instead, she restrained herself, taking her anger out on the floor as she furiously tapped her foot.

"Well, Gail? Brad's coming around. What do you say?" Sam was watching her intently but chose to ignore her temper.

"I say the two of you are either crazy, or you've been hitting the bottle too heavily." She carefully placed her glass on a table. "Good night, gentlemen." She walked out the door in a huff.

Gail stood by the steps for a few minutes, her hand to her chest as she took a deep breath. She didn't believe what she'd just been through. She shook her head and turned to look for a taxi.

"Still here?" Sam's voice startled her.

"Not for long!" she retorted as she waved at a far-off cab.

"Gail, come back in and let's talk some more. If you'll just give it a bit of rational thought, you'll find my idea's a good one. For a lot of reasons."

"Name two."

"I've already named several. Political reasons. Now how about a few personal ones." Sam winked. "He's a helluva catch—you'll be the envy of half the women in America."

"I don't happen to want to be envied, Sam."

"Nonsense. We all enjoy being the object of a little envy. Human nature," Sam chided. "Come on back in. Let's just talk more about it. Discuss it calmly." Gail stood silently. "What do you say?" he persisted. Without waiting for an answer Sam wrapped his arm around her shoulder and gently turned her around. They walked back into the house, Gail unsure why she was returning.

Brad was silent as Sam reiterated all the reasons he and Gail should wed. Gail was also quiet. Speechless might be a better description. She watched Brad sitting casually in an armchair across from her. He had apparently made up his mind. The tenseness was gone from his face. If anything, he appeared to be inwardly smiling at Gail's distress.

She had to admit the idea of being married to Brad wasn't all bad. In a way it was exciting, scary even. But she didn't want to be thrust on anyone; she wanted to be desired, to be romanced, to be loved, not bargained for like some piece of rental property. But what did she really have to lose? Not much. Probably not more than a few months of her time. And Sam was right, there could be gains. Not only political, but it could be a real adventure....

CHAPTER FOUR

GAIL TUNED back into the conversation, although Sam and Brad apparently had the idea that she'd been listening the whole time. No sooner had she agreed to go along with the scheme than Sam was discussing logistics with them. He'd obviously thought this out beforehand.

"You two will elope tonight. Dave will take care of the media," Sam said. "You'll take some time off for a honeymoon." He gestured quotes around the word honeymoon. "Then Brad will come back here to Washington and Gail will go back to Louisiana to do some wifely campaigning." Sam looked at Gail. "You've been effective behind the scenes, getting things organized, but Brad needs a visible presence there full-time while he finishes up work on that bill."

After a half hour more of hurried, intense planning, Gail got up. "I'd better get moving if I'm going to get everything together tonight." She turned to Brad. "Call me when you're ready to go." He looked up and nodded in response. Gail couldn't quite read his expression. She wondered if he was annoyed or agitated or both. Brad had made no secret of his views on marriage. He was probably furious at being trapped into it.

Gail walked outside, escorted by Sam who was cradling her elbow as she stepped toward the curb to search for a taxi. "You know, Sam, maybe this is not such a good idea."

"Then why did you agree to it? Don't fret so, Gail—it'll work out just fine."

"But I have this—this premonition. I think Brad's going to regret having to do this, and when he does, he's going to look for someone to blame. Someone like me."

"Isn't that what wives are for?" Sam chuckled.

"Oh, you. You're a big help," she moaned.

"Calm down, my girl," Sam soothed. "I was just teasing." He patted her shoulder. "Trust me, Gail. My instincts tell me it'll work out better than you think."

"And if it doesn't?"

"Then I'm sure I'll spend the rest of my life hearing about it from you."

"Count on it," she said.

SAM PICKED UP his pipe. "Well, Brad. That girl has real spunk."

Brad laughed bitterly. "She's a young idiot, that's what she is. Going along with a phony marriage when she doesn't even know what marriage is." He reached for his drink on the table and gulped it down.

"And you *do*?" Sam had a slight smile on his face. "Excuse me for being presumptuous, Brad, but don't you have to be married at least once to know what marriage is all about?"

"You've got a short memory, Sam. Maybe I haven't experienced wedded bliss firsthand, but I've sure had a lot of exposure to my mother's."

"I'm sorry, Brad. I know you're bitter about your mother."

"Bitter?" Brad scoffed. "I'm not bitter. I'm just realistic. Marriage is a pact made by two fools who think they are in love. What they don't know is that there is no such thing as love. Love is a fantasy, an illusion that exists for a brief period of time—maybe a week, maybe a year—until the two people begin to really look at each other. Then the true feelings come out."

"Then marriage to Gail will be perfect. Since you're *not* two fools who think they're in love. You won't have to worry about fantasies or illusions."

Brad walked back toward the kitchen. "I need another drink."

"Oh, no you don't," said Sam. The tone of Sam's voice seemed to stop Brad in his tracks. "You've made a deal. Now you go through with it sober."

Brad turned and stood fixated for a few seconds. Then he shrugged his shoulders in a gesture of acquiescence and walked silently toward the front door.

"And one more thing," shouted Sam at Brad's back. "You treat that girl right."

Gail and Brad stood alone in the secluded lounge waiting to board the charter jet Sam had arranged. Brad unwrapped a package of gum and offered Gail a stick. She shook her head and looked away. *I have to do it. I have to get this matter settled now. Before it's too late.* She cleared her throat and turned to Brad. "I suppose I should have brought this up before, but I think now is as good a time as any to discuss it."

"To discuss what?" Brad stuck a piece of gum into his mouth.

"Well," she stared at her feet, then looked up. "Since this marriage will only last until the election is over, I...you...you understand the arrangement will be...uh, platonic."

Brad looked down at her, his eyes darkening. "Have I said or done anything recently to make you think you're in any danger of unwanted attention?"

Gail felt her neck redden, embarrassed at the insulting arrogance in his voice. "No," she purred. "But there's your reputation of jumping on anything female that isn't comatose. And I just wanted to make sure you understand the marriage license doesn't necessarily give *you* license."

Now it was Brad's turn to inflict more barbed words. "Contrary to what you may have heard, my dear wife-to-be," he snarled, "some women are completely safe from my satyrlike ways. And you will be one of those women. You may be sure I won't touch you with or without a ten-foot pole." He gave her a hard stare. "Feel better?"

"Much," she said, keeping her voice as even as possible, in spite of the stabbing pain she suddenly felt. If it weren't for her Meredith stubbornness, she would have fled the terminal then and there. She wanted to. But no way was she going to let this insufferable man know he'd struck a nerve. She was going through with this marriage. She'd keep her end of the bargain. And with any luck, she'd make his life miserable in the process.

By ten o'clock they were airborne, headed toward Juárez, Mexico. Sam had advised against a Washington or Louisiana ceremony as there was too high a risk that the press would get wind of it, something none of them wanted. Sam had a lawyer friend in El Paso, a stone's throw from Juárez, who agreed to arrange a quickie ceremony for the couple that night. There was no waiting period for marriages in Mexico so their plans couldn't be delayed, nor would Brad have a chance to change his mind and back out.

A whirlwind courtship and marriage—it should have been a glamorous and exciting experience. Except that it was a sham, an arrangement, a political rather than a love match. Plus the fact that at that moment both Gail and Brad were dealing with barely-concealed loathing.

Brad had been civil when he escorted Gail onto the plane, but not much else, and as soon as they were seated, he had pulled out his briefcase to do a few hours work. Gail wasn't really surprised at his negative attitude because she felt exactly the same way. After all, they were in identical positions. Both had agreed to this bogus marriage for political reasons and now both were questioning their willingness to go through with it.

Gail stared out at the lights of the myriad small towns and cities they flew over. Was that the only reason she'd agreed to the marriage—for political gain? she wondered.

The wedding itself felt almost surrealistic. They'd landed at El Paso, where a waiting limousine whisked them through the darkened night across the border. Gail felt a multifarious mixture of emotions—fatigue, confusion, excitement, and she could only guess what Brad was thinking. From the looks of him, nothing very pleasant. He was grim and unsmiling. Faint bruises from the encounter which had brought on this hasty marriage were evident around his right eye.

After the ceremony, the couple rode in silence back to El Paso and settled into the bridal suite at a downtown hotel. The suite had two large rooms—a bedroom and a living room area with a couch. Brad gallantly took the couch and explained that he still had work to do. Gail took the bedroom, collapsing into bed after an unbelievably long and complicated day. But, as tired as she was, sleep wouldn't come. She lay awake listening to the street sounds of early morning, wondering what she had let herself in for.

The next morning, after a quick breakfast, they were back on the private plane headed toward Louisiana. Brad had arranged a charter plane to protect them from unwanted press attention when they returned to Louisiana. The announcement wasn't to be released to the media for another twenty-four hours and he preferred to avoid any unscheduled interviews for the time being.

Over breakfast, Brad had tossed her a copy of their agenda for the next week. They were to have a brief honeymoon at Toledo Bend Lake, then drive to Greenbriar before he flew back to Washington. Then, just as casually, he dropped a small box in front of her. "Wear these," he said unfeelingly as Gail opened the delicate velvet case to find two rings, a plain gold wedding band, and a matching engagement ring—a beautiful ruby surrounded by diamond baguettes. She was surprised that Brad had even thought of giving her rings. The man was so unpredictable, she thought.

After they arrived at the Shreveport airport they rented a car and drove the fifty miles to Brad's lakeside cabin. The drive gave Gail a chance to see another side of Louisiana. The terrain was quite different from the southern part of the state. Instead of bridges and bayous and tropical foliage, she saw tall pines, cattle grazing in open fields and farmers working crops.

It was mid-afternoon as they neared the turn-off to the cabin. Brad pulled off the highway onto a hilly dirt road where they bumped their way along, the car brushing against the thick bushes and weeds which bordered the country road. "Well what do you think?" Brad asked, as he stopped the car, the eyebrow over his darkened eye raised in question. "Isn't this place something else?" Brad had that look on his face again—the same one he was wearing when he popped into her apartment. The one that said "The joke's on you."

"Something else," Gail agreed, thinking that this so-called honeymoon was quickly turning into a nightmare.

She looked with dismay at the beat-up old trailer perched on a weed-filled lot. It overlooked the lake, which was close by, big and bare.

Maybe the inside will console me, she hoped, as she followed Brad into the trailer. But there was no consolation to be had. It was strictly a fishing cabin, rods leaning against the walls, fish mounted and hanging in neat rows, with small plaques commemorating the date of the catch, the kind of fish, and, of course, the fisherman who in each case had been Brad. The few pieces of furniture, all utilitarian, were dust covered. Spider webs draped the corners of the room.

"Well, make yourself comfortable," said Brad, a big smile on his face. He looked like a man who had come home from a long journey. Did he really like this place, Gail wondered, or did he select it just to make her miserable? Probably a little bit of both she decided as she looked around. In a way, she was glad this wasn't a real honeymoon. Otherwise, the disappointment would be even more overwhelming.

Gail set about checking the two tiny bedrooms, the bathroom and the small kitchen. Someone had stocked the fridge. It was filled with milk, eggs, fruit, vegetables, colas and a case of beer. The freezer was full, too, with meat, cakes, pastries and two gallons of ice cream. Too bad they hadn't seen fit to clean the place up a bit, she thought, as she ran her fingers across the dusty kitchen cabinets.

"Well, this is it," she said to herself resignedly and went outside to join Brad who was checking the dock.

DAVE HAD BEEN SUMMONED over to Sam's office the morning after the marriage to hear the news and to get information to make the formal announcement to the media.

"Sam, have you gone crazy?" Dave's face showed genuine aggravation.

"What are you talking about?" Sam was wearing his most innocent look.

"Don't try to con me, you old fox. I know who arranged this marriage."

"Have a seat, my boy," said Sam, easing Dave into a chair. "Let's discuss this." He sat down at his desk and began to light up his pipe. "Now, Dave, you know that Brad needed a wife. We discussed it at that strategy session."

"But Gail?" Dave's voice was agitated. Then he answered his own question. "Of course, Gail. Who else but Gail would agree to an arranged, loveless marriage. Gail would jump off the Capitol if it would better serve the campaign—but you?" He stared at Sam, his face crestfallen. "I can't believe you actually aided and abetted the marriage of two people just for political reasons."

Sam leaned back in his chair. "People get married all the time for worse reasons. Look at the divorce rate in this country. Maybe this reason is as good as any. Besides—" he smiled, eyeing Dave over the top of his glasses, "Maybe you don't realize it, and maybe that blockhead Brad doesn't realize it, but Gail is crazy about him."

Dave looked up in shock.

"It's true." Sam went on. "I've seen the expression on her face when she doesn't know anyone is watching. She'll be good for Brad. He needs a nice woman to love him—to make him believe in women again." He puffed long and hard on his pipe. "Yep, she's perfect for him, and sooner or later he'll figure it out himself."

GAIL AND BRAD HAD SETTLED into a little routine by midweek. Actually, it was his routine and Gail did the settling. Brad would have a quick cup of coffee about six a.m., go off fishing, home for a brief lunch, then spend the afternoon working. He had to keep up not only with campaign duties but with his congressional chores as well. Gail was appointed chief cook and bottle washer. She cleaned up the trailer, prepared the meals and even got the honor of cleaning the string of fish Brad caught each day. She spent hours planning the campaign and reading. She also took long walks through the piney woods, enjoying the tranquility of the setting, such a contrast to her fast-paced life in the city. The only other people she saw were in the small fishing boats, which passed by every now and then.

In the evenings the two discussed politics or the campaign or Washington. Brad seemed to enjoy her conversation and each night they lingered for a couple of hours over dinner before returning to their respective rooms for the night. Gail knew the respite had been good for both of them. Brad's eye was healed and he was generally more relaxed. He hadn't snapped at Gail since their wedding night, although she still remembered vividly that crack about the ten-foot pole. Nevertheless, Gail felt more comfortable around him. They were almost becoming friends, she realized.

"How about a walk?" Brad asked as he finished his breakfast coffee.

Gail turned from the sink, surprised. "But what about your fishing? Aren't you going out on the lake today?"

"Nah," he said, "I thought we could do something different this morning. Like bird watching. Or berry picking. How soon can you be ready?"

Gail was ready in a flash, her robe traded in for a pair of jeans and a sweatshirt, her face washed, her ponytail fastened.

They walked through the thick pines, Brad identifying particular flora and fauna along the way. He smiled and pointed to a male blue jay, who was protesting their invasion of his territory.

"Look," she said, pointing to the dark berries.

"Blackberries." He plucked one off the bush and popped it into his mouth. "Try one. They're about ripe."

But before Gail could reach out and pluck one for herself, Brad had already done so, and was raising a particularly luscious one to her lips. "Here," he said softly, his fingertips gently grazing her lips as they parted to accept his offering. It was a strangely sensual action. For a long moment their eyes locked, then Gail looked away shyly.

As they walked, the quietness was penetrated by the sound of machines in the distance. "What's that noise?" Gail asked.

Brad scowled. "It's the lignite company. They're strip mining for coal."

Gail frowned, realizing the import of his statement. "Does that mean this place will become an ugly strip mine?"

"I hope not," Brad sighed. "The plan is to restore the land after it's mined. I just hope the plan is followed—otherwise, these beautiful forests could be turned into an eyesore." The idea seemed to sadden him.

He broke off a piece of pine branch and sniffed it. "That's what makes my proposal so important—protecting our land, our natural resources is so vital. Ah, well...end of speech." He smiled at Gail—not his usual bright contrived political smile, but a sincere grin. "We'd better head on back." He took her hand in his as they maneuvered a fence. But as they continued their walk back to the trailer, he released his grip, letting his hand fall away from hers.

The following morning Brad went out fishing and Gail took another walk. She had hoped Brad might accompany her again but he'd heard the bass were biting so he rushed on out to the boat right after breakfast.

Gail walked about a mile through the woods to the main road, gathering wildflowers from patches by the side of the road. She thought they'd look pretty arranged in a jar on the kitchen counter.

Suddenly she saw a bee hovering around the flowers in her hand. "Scat," she said, flicking at the bee with her free hand. The bee retreated, but came right back—this time to her neck. She could hear the buzzing close to her ear.

Oh no! She'd used a perfumed soap and the scent had diverted the bee's attention from the flowers. Gail dropped the bouquet and swatted at her head knocking her glasses into the tall grass as she did so. The buzzing became louder. There were now two or three bees.

Gail let out a yelp as one of the bees stung her under the earlobe. Then she felt another sting on the neck. And another. She started running toward the cabin, screaming all the way as she raced for the door.

Brad was tying up the boat. He looked up, an expression of alarm on his face as she ran yelling into the cabin. Gail had just grabbed a can of insect spray, ready to do battle when Brad came rushing through the door.

"What's the matter?" he shouted, slightly short of breath having run from the dock. His eyes were filled with concern.

Tears streamed down Gail's face. She fell into his arms, pointing to the red welts on her neck. "Bees. I was afraid the whole hive was going to come after me."

Brad turned her face to the side, his hands gently stroking her soft skin as he examined the wounds. "Looks like three or four got you. Let me see what I can do for that."

He walked over to the cabinet and pulled out a box of baking soda. For the next few minutes, Gail sat quietly while Brad ministered to her bee stings, his presence and gentle touches calming her.

"There. Think that's about got it. An aspirin will probably help too. Are you in much pain?"

Not as much as before, Gail thought, feeling the closeness of Brad's face to her, his breath on her neck. But she nodded.

He looked carefully into her glistening eyes. "I'm glad you're okay. For a moment there..." Brad hesitated, then cupped her face in his hand in a gentle caress. Gail's dark eyes widened in surprise as she looked up at him.

Brad bent down and softly touched his lips to hers. One arm pulled her against his body and he kissed her again. Gail didn't resist. She was too stunned to offer any protest. And she liked the feel of his lips against hers, the press of his strong body, even the stubble of his beard scratching her face. Until it rubbed against her injured neck. "Ohhh," she cried, pushing against him.

Brad pulled back apologetically. "I'm sorry. I guess I've broken our agreement."

"No," she began.

"It's all right," he interrupted. "You don't have to explain." His look was one of calm resignation.

He sure was quick to think the wrong thing, Gail thought. But her neck was throbbing too much now for a discussion. Compliantly she took two aspirin and headed toward the bedroom as Brad went out to look for her glasses.

It was late afternoon before sleep finally overtook her. Even then she slept fretfully, feverish from the bee stings. Fortunately, the pain had been tempered by other stronger feelings generated by Brad's kisses and by his tender concern.

THE CAMARADERIE, which had been establishing itself before the bee incident, was now completely gone. Brad had inquired about her neck the next morning, but since then, there had been no conversation—not about the weather, the campaign, or their marriage. Brad had made only the most perfunctory comments as they packed for the trip south. The drive, a long one, passed in silence. Gail felt tired and disheveled as they stopped the car in the driveway of Brad's country home.

The front door opened and Aunt Sussy flew down the steps toward the car. "I thought I heard someone approaching," she chirped as she hugged Brad and Gail. "Oh, I've been in such a state since I got the phone call about your marriage. Oh!" she hugged her hands to her chest. "I'm so excited for you."

Gail laughed in spite of herself as she and Aunt Sussy walked up the steps, leaving Brad and Calvin to handle the luggage. Aunt Sussy's enthusiasm made the marriage seem almost real. *I'd hate for her to discover the truth,* Gail thought, *if the illusion makes her so happy.*

Brad joined them in the foyer just in time for his aunt to say, "I've got the master suite all ready for you. Do you want to go freshen up before lunch?" Aunt Sussy had a twinkle in her eye as though she expected more than freshening up.

Gail began to protest but was stopped by Brad who pulled her quickly toward him, his arm around her waist. "Thanks, you old turnip," he said lovingly. "We'll be down before long."

They were halfway up the stairs, out of Aunt Sussy's earshot, when Brad stopped to glare at Gail. "I don't want her to think this marriage is anything but real. It would be confusing and unsettling for her. And embarrassing for me,'' he added. The harsh tone of his voice captured Gail's attention and she looked up at him questioningly. ''While we're here, *Mrs. Harrison*, you'll pretend to be the loving and happy bride—okay?'' He obviously intended no argument, his hand tightening around her waist as he led her into a large bedroom.

Gail glanced about the lovely room. A fireplace surrounded by blue mosaic tiles graced one wall. There was a sitting area with a love seat, French bouillotte lamps and an antique highboy. Fragrances from fresh-cut flowers permeated the room, which was dominated by a massive four-poster bed covered with a creamy lace spread.

Brad left his arm on her waist for several moments after he'd closed the bedroom door, as though he was trying to decide what to do with her. Finally, he released her with a jerk. ''The bathroom's through there—come down when you're finished.'' He left the room, almost colliding with the servant bringing up their luggage.

Gail looked around, wondering if there was an adjoining parlor where Brad intended to sleep—or for her to sleep. But the only door led to the bathroom and dressing areas. She managed a smile as she thought of Brad, miserable, his large form doubled up on the small, fragile love seat. But he'd have to sleep there. If not, that left only the bed and . . . her eyes widened, drawn there as if by command. Did Brad really intend to share that bed with her? How far would he carry this charade?

An hour later, the three were seated at the dining table, Aunt Sussy chattering cheerfully as Crystal served the meal. Brad put his arm around Crystal as he introduced her to Gail, explaining that she'd been with the Harrison family since his childhood and was the best cook in Louisiana. The meal she prepared confirmed his statement, but Gail's nerves had never been so taut, and she had to feign enthusiasm for the food.

Crystal served a thick cream of onion soup, shrimp salad, crusty French bread and chilled champagne. For dessert, much to Gail's dismay, she brought out a three-layered wedding cake decorated with tiny spun-sugar doves and on the top tier, a ceramic bride and groom.

"Isn't she wonderful," Brad waxed enthusiastically as he rose from the table and kissed Crystal on the cheek. Then he went over to Gail and handed her the ribbon-trimmed silver server, gently closing his hand over hers as they cut the cake together. Brad took a small piece and fed it to Gail, surprising her by the traditional action. More of the cake went on her face than in her mouth and he leaned over, nibbling the crumbs off her cheek, much to Aunt Sussy's delight. Gail was mesmerized by the situation, by his touch. She stood motionless until Brad's voice summoned her attention. "Well?" he asked, gesturing toward the cake. So, at his bidding she picked up a small piece and fed it to him.

After a toast to their happiness by Aunt Sussy, Brad had Crystal call in the entire staff for cake and more champagne. Brad was warm and charming with his staff; they seemed more his friends than his servants. His warmth was different from the kind he displayed as a politician—it seemed more genuine. Even the way he was acting toward Gail seemed somehow real. For he never left her side. He held her hand, kissed her cheek several times and made a thoroughly convincing show for the group. But Gail knew the adoring bridegroom role was just a pretense.

When lunch was over, Brad suggested to Aunt Sussy that she show Gail around the grounds while he adjourned to his study to catch up on some paperwork. Aunt Sussy was only too willing to share this lovely setting with her nephew's wife and to make her feel at home.

Gail knew she would have to keep reminding herself her sojourn at Greenbriar was only temporary. The place was so beautiful, so comfortable. She had a good feeling about it. It would take little effort to fall in love with the house—and with the people.

Aunt Sussy. The woman was a marvel, Gail thought, her outlook on life so contemporary, her enthusiasm so youthful. She took Gail from room to room, then out the French doors and into the gardens behind the house, chattering happily as she recounted the home's history, occasionally touching the younger woman's arm affectionately, making Gail feel so at home. "And that's the quick tour. We'll do a more extensive one tomorrow." She smiled as they reentered the house.

"You mean there's more?"

"Much more—that was merely a preview. This is a working plantation, Gail. There aren't too many of them left. And since you're now its mistress, you need to know all about the operations. Particularly since Brad has to spend so much time in Washington." She patted Gail's hand. "Now, if you'll excuse me, I'd better check the kitchen and see what Crystal's doing about supper." She walked through the foyer, heels clicking on the bare floor.

Gail headed upstairs. Just as her hand clasped the railing of the circular staircase, she stopped, hearing voices coming from Brad's study. She listened for a moment. Gail knew that voice—a female voice. Quietly, she tiptoed toward the study. The door was slightly ajar, and through the crack she could see Judith DeWitt sitting on the arm of Brad's chair. She was facing him, one hand resting on his shoulder. "But, darling, if you wanted to get married, we could have worked something out," she laughed. Gail couldn't hear Brad's mumbled response. But she could see Judith's lips nearing his as she told him, "Well, congratulations, I guess. And if you ever need anything, remember New Orleans isn't far away."

Gail turned and rushed up the stairs, not wanting to hear anymore, or worse, witness a love scene. It served her right, she told herself. She shouldn't have been eavesdropping. But that didn't stop the tears from rolling down her cheeks, the pain from stirring in her heart.

The sun was setting on the horizon when Brad joined her in their bedroom. Gail had curled up by the window, a folder of campaign material in her lap. She sat there motionless, her tears gone, a strange melancholy enveloping her.

"I thought you were taking a nap," Brad said. He sat down on the love seat and stretched his legs out in front of him.

"I was talking with Aunt Sussy," he continued. "We think you need a little time to get adjusted to all this rather than just jumping out on the campaign trail with me, cold. A short stay here at the plantation to help get your thoughts together will be good for you and it'll give me a chance to finish some matters in Washington. Maybe by then, the brouhaha in the press will have died down a bit and you won't be swamped by reporters. They've apparently heard we're back—a few came by here this afternoon. Aunt Sussy put them off as only she could do it." He smiled thoughtfully. "What do you say?"

"I say my opinion could hardly matter," Gail snapped. "And was it you and Aunt Sussy—or maybe you and Judith DeWitt—who put this plan together? You said earlier, Brad, that you didn't want to be embarrassed by this—this mockery. Well, I don't relish being the brunt of any jokes either. The new bride has already been cheated on."

Brad's smile froze and his eyes became an ice blue. "I think I'd better make it clear that I will call the shots, Gail. This is my campaign, not yours. And I don't need any more headaches. So you can just eliminate the jealousy bit and plan on a relaxing stay here." He rose to leave.

"Wait a minute. That's ridiculous. The whole purpose of this farce was to show Brad Harrison as the happily married family man—trot out the little wife and all that. What good can I possibly be, cooling my heels here? I should be working. I'd rather be working."

"And I'd rather you stayed here for now. I need a breather to—to adjust to having a bride."

Gail was skeptical. "To adjust to being married...or to give you time to have a fling with Judith?"

"What's this jealousy bit about Judith? She's like a sister to me. You know, Gail, for all the brains Sam credits you with having, occasionally you're just plain stupid. If there was anything romantic between Judith and me, I'd have married her a long time ago. Remember, I married to erase my playboy image. Do you honestly think I'm dumb enough to trade it in on a philandering husband one? No, my dear, the name of the game is fidelity—and it'd better damn well be that way for you too! Don't think I'm not aware of what's going on between you and Dave." He crossed the room and pulled the door open. "I'll see you soon." The door slammed loudly behind him.

By the time Gail recovered her composure, Brad was already leaving. She was coming down the stairs when she saw him take Judith's arm and walk out the front door. She returned to her room, slammed the door after her as hard as Brad had, and fell onto the bed. Her anger brought back the bitter tears and she lay sobbing. It wasn't long before emotional and physical exhaustion finally overtook her and she succumbed to a restless sleep.

The open drapes revealed a dark sky as Gail woke to a tapping on the door. "Come in," she mumbled in her drowsiness and Aunt Sussy entered with a tray balanced on one hand.

"I hope you don't mind my waking you, dear, but I was rather worried about you." She set the tray down on a table and came over to the bed. "Gail—oh, dear, have you been crying?" She took Gail's hand in hers and patted it gently. "You have been crying," she accused. "What did Bradley do? Oh," she paused, "he left with Judith, didn't he?" She looked directly into Gail's eyes, the look confirming her statement.

"I know what you're thinking, but you're wrong," Aunt Sussy comforted. "You don't need to worry about Judith. They're really just old friends. Bradley's known her for years and if they wanted to marry each other—well, they've had plenty of chances. Now get out of that bed and come have some tea." She walked over to the table and started pouring from the china teapot. "Gail, dear, every time you start feeling blue, just remember—he married *you*."

"But he didn't," Gail protested.

"You're not married?" Aunt Sussy looked astonished.

"Yes, yes, we're married—but it's—it's just a setup," Gail confessed. "To help Brad out politically. He didn't want to marry me." She sat up, wrapping her arms around her knees and stared down at the floor.

Aunt Sussy watched Gail thoughtfully. "But what about you? Did you want to marry him?"

"Not at first."

"Well then, why did you? What did you have to gain—unless maybe you do care a little bit about my nephew."

Gail dabbed at her eyes with her napkin. "You mean that conceited, arrogant, abrasive, selfish oaf?" she asked indignantly as she sniffed a couple of times. "Well I don't,"

"Gail," Aunt Sussy sounded like a mother who'd caught her child fibbing.

Gail lowered her head again and mumbled a reply. "Oh, I don't know. Maybe I do."

Aunt Sussy reached over and took her chin, lifting her face up. "Gail, Bradley would never marry anyone unless he wanted to. I know him too well. I'd always worried he wouldn't marry at all or that he would—would marry a whirligig like his mother. You can't imagine how pleased I was when I heard the news you two had eloped. You're just perfect for him. He has a very jaded view of marriage, you know." She handed Gail a cup of tea. "Sugar, lemon?"

"Both," Gail nodded. She pondered Aunt Sussy's statement as she stirred her tea. "It's obvious how he feels about marriage. But I don't know why."

By way of explanation, the older woman waved her hand, taking in the room and the rest of the house and grounds in the gesture. "This looks like a setting for total tranquility, doesn't it, dear? But on two occasions, it's been a battleground. First, during The War Between the States, when Union troops passed through, and second, during Bradley's childhood, when his parents battled constantly. He was only nine when his mother finally left— ran off with another man, one of her many lovers and husbands. His father eventually drank himself to death over Genevieve's escapades, and I took over care of Bradley. Luckily, we hit it off so well. His father was useless, wallowing in self-pity, and his mother flitted back in and out of his life like a hummingbird. The only stability he knew was this house and me—and now he has you. I know how difficult he can be at times, Gail, but don't give up on him. My nephew needs you, whether he knows it or not.''

"Was his mother very beautiful?" Gail whispered.

"Very," Aunt Sussy confirmed.

"So I am perfect for him then," Gail scoffed. "He won't have to worry about a plain wife running away. Anyway," she continued, "it doesn't really matter because Brad won't have me on any long-term basis, anyway."

"So," Aunt Sussy asked matter-of-factly, "what are you going to do about it?"

"What do you mean? What can I do about it?" Gail said in a subdued tone of voice.

"Don't look so dejected—" Aunt Sussy reached over to pat Gail's hand "—it's not hopeless. All Bradley needs is a lot of encouragement, and a little more time—time to fall in love."

"That's a laugh," Gail said. "How can I even get his attention with Judith DeWitt chauffeuring him around and purring into his ear all the time. She's so sexy and gorgeous, I feel like a gnome by comparison."

"Now you just stop that talk," admonished Aunt Sussy. She slapped the love seat firmly with her hand. "You're every bit as pretty as Judith or any of those other assorted women he's been with."

Gail shot Aunt Sussy a wary look.

"I mean it." Aunt Sussy leaned on her elbow to study Gail closely. "With the right clothes and makeup, you could be stunning." She fingered the ponytail Gail had hastily secured earlier. "And a new hairdo wouldn't hurt either. You're twenty-seven years old. You might as well start looking your age."

Gail looked up at Aunt Sussy skeptically but there was hope in her voice. "Do you really think I could be 'stunning'?"

"A smasher!" insisted Aunt Sussy.

"But I—I wouldn't know where to begin."

"Sure you would. You just need a little push. I'll tell you what." She patted Gail's cheek. "You concentrate on the Bradley Harrison campaign and let me be the manager of the Gail Harrison campaign."

CHAPTER FIVE

THE NEXT WEEK Gail was thrown into a frenzy of activity like she had never before experienced. Even the last days of a hard-fought political campaign couldn't compare with the work Aunt Sussy had cut out for her. Early on Gail's first morning at Greenbriar, Aunt Sussy explained the plan of action. They would be leaving for New Orleans after breakfast to put the plan into effect.

As Gail sipped black coffee and munched on dry toast, Aunt Sussy recounted the story in the morning newspaper about the "mysterious" Mrs. Harrison. "And we want to keep up that aura of mystery," she said, handing Gail the newspaper. All the article said was that Congressman Harrison's staff wouldn't reveal any detailed information about his new bride, but the congressman would answer any questions during his appearance on *America AM* the next morning. It went on to say that Brad would be returning to Louisiana for campaign appearances soon, and that Mrs. Harrison would be accompanying her husband to these functions. "The new Mrs. Harrison is indeed a woman of mystery."

Gail looked up at Aunt Sussy and shook her head. "Never in a thousand years would I have dreamed I could be referred to as a 'woman of mystery.'" She laughed. "But one thing is certain, my appearance will remain a mystery as they'll never find a picture of me—having my picture taken is something I've always avoided. I even escaped the high school and college yearbooks—I don't think I've had as much as a snapshot taken since I was about ten or eleven.''

"But, why, dear? Pictures serve as nice mementos and they're fun to look at, especially when you're my age.''

Gail grimaced. ''I guess I didn't want anyone capturing my double chin.''

"You don't have a double chin! I just don't understand why you're so sensitive about your appearance—and why you don't play up your beauty. As I keep telling you, you're a lovely looking woman. Those luminous brown eyes and nice high cheekbones. Why once you get a new hairdo and some fashionable clothes, you'll have Bradley fighting off half the men in Louisiana.'' She paused for a few moments, as if in deep thought. ''Gail, how can a woman with your intelligence have such a negative self-image? Was it growing up without a mother?'' She gave Gail an inquiring look that demanded a reply.

With Aunt Sussy's encouragement, Gail's story tumbled out. She explained how she'd been a chubby youngster who was always the class brain, not a popular combination. She became a shy teenager who was asked out by young men because they thought they might get a foot up the political ladder by meeting her father, a senator from Oklahoma. She grew into a young woman trying to please only her father, and to avoid more pain by absorbing herself totally in politics to the exclusion of all else, including personal relationships.

All the old hurts were revealed as she opened up to Aunt Sussy. It was the first time in her life she'd really discussed her feelings with anyone, and it became apparent that Aunt Sussy was not only going to be her Svengali, but also her Sigmund Freud. ''Now, dear, you already know you can manage a state-wide political campaign,'' Aunt

Sussy pointed out. "Well, if you can handle that you can also handle being Mrs. Bradley Harrison. You are a worthy, competent, beautiful woman. You just need to give your looks as much attention as your work."

She sighed. "But that's enough preaching. We've got to be going." Aunt Sussy rose from the table. "Frankly," she giggled, "I'm glad you had such an aversion to pictures—the more of an enigma you are, the more fun this is going to be!" Gail was dubious about the whole plan. "And, another thing," encouraged Aunt Sussy, undaunted, "the more publicity it will bring to the campaign.

"Oh, speaking of the campaign, you had a call from Dave McElroy while you were dressing. He's in New Orleans."

"Dave? How wonderful," Gail said. "I can't wait to talk to him. I'm dying for some news. Ever since I became Mrs. Harrison, I've been out of touch with the day-to-day operations of the campaign." Gail suddenly realized how much she missed being involved.

"Aunt Sussy, do you mind if I stop by campaign headquarters this morning before we hit the shops?" All Gail really knew about the campaign was the sparse information provided by the newspapers and television. Other than the public's curiosity about her identity, she wasn't sure what her marriage to Brad had accomplished. Perhaps Dave had some answers.

"Of course not," Aunt Sussy said, "it will give me some time to organize Brad's town house where you and I can stay for a few days while we put our plan into action."

"Thanks, Aunt Sussy, I knew you'd understand."

DAVE LOOKED UP from his reading as Gail entered the little office in the back of the campaign headquarters. "Gail!" He came around the desk. "Can I kiss the new bride?'' Without waiting for an answer, he hugged Gail and gave her a quick kiss on the lips.

They smiled self-consciously at each other, a little embarrassed at their reunion. ''Well come sit down,'' he said, pulling a chair up for her, ''and tell me all about it.''

Gail smiled. ''Dave. I don't know what to say.'' She smiled. ''I guess you could say it's been quite a week.'' They both laughed. She told him about the wedding in Juárez and the trip to Toledo Bend Lake, describing the fishing and the food and the scenery, carefully omitting any mention of her relationship with Brad. ''And I just drove in from the plantation this morning. Aunt Sussy is in town, too. I dropped her off at Brad's town house.''

''Aunt Sussy? Terrific! I'd love to see her again.''

''Well then let's get together. How about dinner tonight?''

Dave quickly accepted the invitation and the two of them spent the rest of the morning going over the latest poll results and scheduling activities for the week. Brad's drop in the polls had leveled off since the marriage, but it was evident a lot of ground had to be regained to make up for the plummet caused by the incident at the Georgetown restaurant.

''Brad said you aren't to be directly involved in any campaigning until he gets down here. What do you plan to do with all that leisure time?'' Dave asked, snapping closed the folder of campaign material.

''Well, for one thing I'm going to purchase some clothes befitting a congressman's wife. And after that,'' said Gail, ''I'll hire a fairy godmother for a complete makeover.''

''Bullcorn,'' said Dave, ''you look great just as you are.''

Gail gave Dave a grateful smile. You are one sweet man, she thought.

At noon, Gail left the headquarters to pick up Aunt Sussy and to embark on the campaign to change plain Gail Meredith into stunning Gail Harrison.

First stop on the afternoon agenda was the hairdresser. On Aunt Sussy's orders, Gail's ponytail holder was thrown into the trash can. "I hope never to see that ponytail again," Aunt Sussy twitted as the snipping began. Gail's fine straight hair was trimmed into a shoulder length blunt cut, parted on the side. A conditioner added a soft, silky sheen and highlighting subtly changed the dark blond hair into a lively golden color.

"Wow!" said Aunt Sussy as she viewed the results.

Gail smiled shyly, "Do you really like it?"

"Like it? I love it. But we have no time to dally." She grabbed Gail's arm and hustled her out of the hair salon toward a cosmetic shop three doors down.

Gail's glasses were removed as the makeup artist, Alice, began her work. "Hmmm. Good lines."

After a thorough cleansing and moisturizing, Alice began to apply an ivory foundation, blusher and then a light dusting of face powder. Gail's brown eyes were accented with a mocha eye pencil and eye shadow, and dark mascara was applied to her long, thick lashes.

"I've before me a beautiful woman," said the makeup artist, standing back to admire her handiwork.

"Amazing," cooed Aunt Sussy in agreement.

All Gail could see was a blurry reflection in the mirror; she groped for her glasses. She slipped the frames on and stared. Who was that stranger staring back? The one with the flawless skin, the high cheekbones and the brown eyes dramatic even through the thick lenses? "Is that me?" she gasped, unable to stifle a smile.

"It's you, dear." Aunt Sussy placed her hands on Gail's shoulders. "And you are beautiful.... However," she frowned as she stepped back to take in the whole image, "what do you think about getting some contact lenses?"

Gail looked up at the makeup artist. "Next week she'll have me in surgery for a nose job," she laughed.

"Hmmm," said Aunt Sussy as she tweaked Gail's nose. "Maybe a little off the sides." She smiled.

"Oh, no you don't," interrupted the makeup artist. "No one's operating on that gorgeous face."

Gorgeous? Gail was flattered, although she knew it was an exaggeration. But no time to think about that. Aunt Sussy was now ready for the department stores.

By the time she and Aunt Sussy met Dave for dinner, Gail was pooped. They were seated at Antoine's having a drink, Gail's new shoes lying under the table as she rubbed her swollen feet against each other.

"I don't know how you do it," she gasped to Aunt Sussy. "You look fresh as a daisy and I'm about to fall out of my chair in exhaustion. I feel like we've gone to half the clothing stores in New Orleans."

Aunt Sussy patted her arm. "But it was worth it, dear. You needed a new wardrobe for your new look." Aunt Sussy took a sip of her gin and tonic. "Ah, just what the doctor ordered."

"Just what the doctor ordered," echoed Gail as she eyed Aunt Sussy's drink and looked down at her glass of club soda and lime. "Low-cal bubbling water. Oh, there's Dave." She waved to him across the room, but Dave didn't appear to see her. He kept glancing around the room. She waved again but to no avail. "He's playing coy," she said as she left the table and walked over to him.

"For Pete's sake, Dave, what does a girl have to do to get your attention?"

Dave stared for a moment. "Good God! Is that you, Gail?"

Gail laughed. "Of course it's me—the new me.

"It's unbelievable! You look like a different person." He followed her to the table.

"Aunt Sussy. My favorite girl!" he exclaimed giving her a kiss on the cheek. "You've got a new look too. No wonder I didn't recognize you girls."

Aunt Sussy smoothed the back of her head. "Just a new hairdo for me since I last saw you. But Gail's the one with the new look."

"I'll say," he agreed. He studied Gail's face.

"Well," Gail asked self-consciously. "Do you like it?"

His voice was thoughtful. "Yes," he said hesitantly as he nodded his head. "I like it. But I'm not sure I like it better. I really liked you the way you were."

"Isn't that something," grumbled Gail kiddingly to Aunt Sussy. "Is it possible to please a man?"

But Aunt Sussy didn't return her look. Instead she gazed at Dave, a thoughtful expression on her face.

After they'd bade Dave good-night, Aunt Sussy said, "That man's in love with you, Gail."

"Oh sure," Gail laughed. But the look in Aunt Sussy's eyes told her she wasn't joking. "You're serious," she said.

"Yes I am," nodded Aunt Sussy. "I only hope Bradley won't notice it."

"I'm afraid he already has—not that he cares anyway," said Gail dejectedly.

THE TWO WOMEN were up early the next morning, television tuned in to *America AM*. They'd stayed at the town house in the city for convenience. Brad was sitting across from the show's hostess, Agnes O'Malley. He looked as handsome as ever, and perfectly confident.

"Good morning, Congressman."

"Hi Agnes," his deep voice vibrated.

"Congressman Harrison, everyone loves a lover so they say. And you've certainly set Washington—and Louisiana—abuzz with your recent marriage."

Brad smiled, his toothy political smile. "And I thought I was here to discuss issues."

"Oh no," she flirted. "Where did you ever get that idea? No, you're here to be chastised. First, for keeping your new bride such a secret, and second, for blowing the cover story of *Newsday* magazine right out of the water." She picked up the copy of *Newsday* with Brad's picture gracing the cover. The caption read: Washington's Most Eligible Bachelor. "By the time this story hit the newsstands, Congressman, you were a married man!" Her tone was playful but slightly mocking.

Brad chuckled softly. "But I do understand the issue sold well. Perhaps that will help the people at *Newsday* forgive me."

"You have a point," Agnes agreed. "Now, tell us about your new wife."

"Well," Brad crossed his legs and smiled, "Gail has been involved in politics all her life. Her father, Russell Meredith, was a well-respected senator. She's a special woman, very intelligent, and we're very much in love...."

"Humph!" Gail muttered. "If he loses the election, he can fall back on his acting ability."

Aunt Sussy gave her a cross look, "Sssh!"

Brad was looking directly into the camera, his eyes communicating intimately with each viewer. "She has a rare inner beauty that few women possess."

"That's just another way of saying I don't look like much on the outside," Gail said grimly.

"Now you just hush up," scolded Aunt Sussy. "That wasn't what he said at all."

"Congressman," the interviewer probed, "it must be difficult to be so far apart so soon after your marriage. Mrs. Harrison is in Louisiana, isn't she?"

Brad flashed another toothy grin at the woman sitting next to him. "I promised Gail a little while to rest up." He leaned back in his chair. "After all, the honeymoon was rather tiring." He paused. "So as much as I'd like to keep her all to myself when I return to Louisiana—I suppose I'll relent and share her with you. But just a little," he drawled in an exaggerated Southern accent.

Gail's face was red hot. Never in all her life had she felt so embarrassed. Brad implying such nonsense about their marriage on national television. She was furious.

She told Brad so when he telephoned the town house later to ask how she and Aunt Sussy were faring in New Orleans. Brad cut her off curtly. "I thought the whole purpose of this charade was to make everyone believe I am besotted with you. Well, I'll handle my role as I see fit— you need only be concerned with your part of the bargain!" He hung up before she could manage a retort.

Within moments the telephone rang again. It was Brad. "I'm sorry...for hanging up and for embarrassing you. Actually, I was enjoying myself and just said the first thing I thought of. I didn't mean to be clever at your expense."

Gail was startled by the apology but still annoyed. "Well, that's exactly what you were doing. And I refuse to be used like that again."

"Okay, okay," he said. "I goofed. But I guess there's not much I can do about it now, is there?"

"No," she grumbled. "Live television is hard to undo."

"By the way," Brad said, changing the subject, "I saw Sam yesterday."

The mention of Sam caused Gail to forget her irritation. "I haven't talked to him since—since before the wedding. I miss him."

"Why don't you give him a call, then?"

"You wouldn't mind?"

"I'm not a ogre, Gail. Although you apparently think so. Maybe some day you'll see I have one or two redeeming qualities. Though I should live so long," he added cynically. "Goodbye." And he hung up.

The two women hit the stores again that morning, walking from boutique to boutique searching for new outfits for the congressman's wife. Gail never realized shopping could be such fun or that stylish clothing could make such a difference to one's appearance. But Aunt Sussy's enthusiasm was catching. "Let's go look at the designer section," the older woman insisted.

Gail registered a shocked look. "Those prices are outrageous. Besides, how are the voters going to relate to designer clothes?"

"They're going to relate just fine," said Aunt Sussy all knowingly. "Being in fashion has never hurt. Look at Jacqueline Kennedy and Nancy Reagan."

Gail knew better than to argue. Obediently, she followed Brad's aunt up the escalator to the designer boutique on the second floor of the department store.

Within three hours Gail had acquired enough clothes to outfit a ladies' club. Day wear, evening wear, cocktail dresses, two suits, four blouses, three skirts, plus belts and shoes. "Let's eat," gasped Gail. "I'm starving."

"Right," agreed Aunt Sussy. "Lunch, and then an appointment with the ophthalmologist."

"Another appointment," repeated Gail. "How wonderful."

"Don't be sarcastic, my dear," chided Aunt Sussy. "It doesn't become a senator's wife." She winked at Gail.

"Yes, ma'am," said Gail mockingly. "I'll try to remember."

GAIL'S HANDS WERE TREMBLING as she sprayed a fine floral mist on her neck and wrists. She walked across the master bedroom and stood in front of the floor-length antique mirror. She'd had three days to get used to her new look, but she still could hardly believe the image in front of her. Even her glasses were gone, replaced by contact lenses. She wondered how Brad would react.

He didn't know she was planning to meet him at the airport—she hadn't told anyone but Aunt Sussy. It was not to be a public welcome; the press had not been informed of Brad's arrival time. Her hands were damp as she gripped the steering wheel. She hoped Brad wouldn't be angered by a surprise greeting from his remodeled wife. She bit her lower lip nervously as she maneuvered Brad's dark green Porsche into the parking space outside the terminal.

Gail glanced at her watch. The plane was to land in ten minutes. She smoothed the skirt of her red-and-white pinstriped dress, straightening the wide red belt as she walked across the tiled floor of the terminal. She wasn't aware that several men had turned to look admiringly.

The gate was crowded with people but Gail had no trouble spotting Brad immediately as he stepped through the door. She walked forward tremulously—he seemed to be looking for someone. Oh no, she thought, what if Judith is meeting him? But then she glimpsed Dave making his way through the crowd toward Brad. He hadn't spotted her. Just as he was grabbing Brad's hand warmly in greeting, Dave glanced over and saw Gail. He smiled and waved to her and at the same time whispered in Brad's ear.

The two men hurried toward her and the next thing Gail knew she was enveloped in Brad's arms. He was holding her so tightly she could hardly breathe. Then his lips were crushing hers in a passionate kiss. As Brad gently released her, Gail could see a television camera crew approaching. "Darling!" he said loudly, "how wonderful of you to come out and meet me." Then he pulled her to him and kissed her again, a kiss as ardent as the first one. He pressed his lips against her forehead, her cheeks and back quickly to her lips, then held her at arm's length, gazing into her eyes. "I've missed you, sweetheart," he whispered, just loudly enough for the nearby sound crew to hear.

His arm went around Gail's waist guiding her through the crush of spectators. A television newswoman shoved a microphone toward them. "Congressman, will you introduce us to Mrs. Harrison?"

"Certainly." He smiled, casting his eyes down at Gail. "My wife, Gail." He pulled her even closer. "No questions tonight, gang," he pleaded. "I'm racing home to be alone with my bride." He squeezed Gail's waist and gave her a big smile. "After all, we're still on our honeymoon."

The crew let them pass. Brad maintained his hold on Gail until they were outside and headed for the car. Once they were alone he released her. "What have you done to yourself?"

"Oh a little of this and that."

He stared at her, the scrutiny taking in her whole body. Gail felt a slight shiver at his appraisal. His eyes returned to hers. His expression indicated to Gail that he found the change interesting. But his words said something else.

"Why did you show up unannounced—you should know better, Gail."

Had she actually expected him to say something nice? How foolish of her, she mused. "I just thought—well, that you—oh never mind what I thought."

"Well just make damn sure you don't ever do something so stupid again." Gail saw his anger in the swift movement before he lifted her by the waist bringing her mouth level with his. Their lips met in a long, sensual kiss, Gail's arms involuntarily circling Brad's neck.

"Hey, you two," Dave interrupted as he came up, luggage in hand, to join them. "We'd better get out of here while the getting is good. You keep carrying on like that and the press will be flocking around in no time."

"Right," Brad agreed, slowing lowering Gail to her feet. "Let's go home and have a look at those informal polls you've been taking. Is the fund-raising really going as badly as you've said?" He and Dave sat in the front of the car talking business, leaving Gail cramped in the back with the luggage.

Brad ignored Gail completely except for an occasional glance in the rearview mirror. Feeling frustrated and left out, Gail finally moved forward and leaned on the backs of their seats, her head jutting between them as they tried to talk. "I supervised a couple of those polls myself," she interrupted, "and they were real eye-openers." Before either man could respond, Gail began relating her findings and she continued talking the rest of the drive home.

When they arrived at the town house, Brad asked Dave to join him in the study, excluding Gail as he closed the door behind them. Gail didn't understand Brad's behavior at all. It was bad enough to be relegated to the back seat, but to be deliberately shut out from the strategy session when not long before she was state campaign manager was a low blow. Gail impatiently paced the floor outside the study, debating whether to burst in uninvited. No, not this time, she decided. She'd just take a brief walk and get some fresh air.

The town house was in shadows by the time Gail returned, the study door still closed. Aunt Sussy came scurrying out of the kitchen. "There you are, dear." She patted Gail's shoulder. "I heard you all come in, but I couldn't find you when I came downstairs. I've been waiting for you to get back so I could leave." She picked up her purse and kissed Gail on the cheek. "I'm going to spend the evening with friends." Gail started to protest only to be stopped by Aunt Sussy. "You and Bradley need some time alone, dear. Now just go on into the kitchen and have something to eat. I've left some things in the refrigerator. I'll see you in the morning."

Gail was too miserable to eat so she didn't even try. Instead she poured a glass of iced tea and took it to the bedroom. She began gathering her things to move across the hall to the guest room, then stopped. Why should she move just to accommodate him? She defiantly threw her belongings back into the drawer. "Let him sleep in there!" she barked and turned toward the bathroom.

After a long soak in a bubble bath, Gail slipped on one of the new nightgowns she'd purchased. It was a diaphanous silvery-blue creation, held onto her shoulders by two silky ribbons. The low cut showed off her well-formed shoulder blades and cream-colored, satiny skin. She sat at the dressing table and brushed her hair, until it shone in a golden halo.

Gail tried not to think about Brad, she tried to feel angry with him, but nothing would work. As much as she hated to admit it, this marriage had become very important to her. It hurt her to think that nothing had changed for him. She was only a convenience, a plastic throwaway to discard when she'd served her purpose. If she'd only realized, that a new Gail wouldn't stand any more of a chance with Brad than the old Gail then maybe she wouldn't be feeling so down. But she'd believed that if she'd just changed her appearance then she'd have a chance with Brad Harrison, a man she couldn't put out of her thoughts. But she was wrong. He'd never want her.

It was nearly midnight when Gail was awakened from a fitful sleep by the bedroom door opening and closing. She could see Brad silhouetted against the window as he removed his clothing, could hear his shoes dropping onto the carpet. She lay silently, feigning sleep, as the comforter was pulled back and the bed sank with Brad's weight. For several minutes he was still, then she could feel his lips brush her shoulder gently. As she opened her eyes and turned toward him, he moved his lips to hers, kissing her softly, then more aggressively. His arms were around her and Gail responded to his embrace, the pain of his earlier rejection forgotten in the wake of the passionate feelings aroused from this unexpected lovemaking.

He pressed his entire length against her, his hard body demanding more than just kisses. She could feel his muscular chest through her silky gown, and shivers of emotion charged through her body as deft fingers untied the ribbons holding up her gown.

GAIL LAY quietly, listening to his breathing. A mixture of emotions tumbled in her mind—excitement, fear, love and, yes, lust. Being held, being kissed so passionately by Brad only whetted her appetite for more. His every move, his every touch had been electrifying. She reached over to touch his arm, but he seemed almost to pull away and suddenly he rose from the bed. He walked over to a small liquor cart, pouring a generous amount of whiskey into a glass.

Gail watched him in the shadows of the darkened room, stunned by his dramatic change in mood. He reminded her of a Greek god standing there, seemingly oblivious to his nudity. Why, she wondered, did he have to ruin this special time by walking away? Did he require an audience to express his feelings? Why had he been so loving, so affectionate? Gail didn't have an answer.

Brad was watching her, a strange look she couldn't decipher in the dark. Suddenly he set down his drink, grabbed his pants from across a chair, and left the room.

Gail had never felt so confused, so miserable.

He had already gone when she awoke the next morning. She paced the floor for a time, then called the campaign headquarters. According to Dave, Brad had been there but had left to take care of some personal business. Gail was certain that the personal business was an excuse to get away from her, to avoid any more contact.

Dave explained that he and Brad were to meet in the afternoon to devise new strategies for replacing the fast-dwindling campaign coffers. He told her Brad was probably out right now making personal appeals for funds. Gail wasn't convinced. Money was a problem for most politicians, but it seemed the campaign always offered her husband a handy excuse whenever he chose to escape. And that's what he was doing now—fleeing from her and from their relationship.

She studied herself in the mirror. Her translucent skin showed dark shadows from the restless night. Why of all days did today have to be Gail's debut as Mrs. Brad Harrison? How would she ever get through this day with a tormented heart and a face to match? A soft tapping at the door interrupted her thoughts.

"Gail, dear, are you ready?" Aunt Sussy stuck her head in the door. "Why you haven't even begun to dress!"

Gail turned around. "Do you think I could just cover my face with a paper sack?"

"Now you just stop that," admonished Aunt Sussy. She moved closer to Gail and peered into her face. "Hmmm. You do look a little worn out. That I will admit, but let's see what we can do." She moved toward the door. "I'll be right back."

In a few minutes she returned, a plate of cucumbers in one hand and a cup of tea in the other. "These are for your eyes," she said, "and this—" she handed the cup to Gail "—is for your disposition. You just lean back in the chaise lounge and let them both go to work on you."

Within an hour, Gail felt as if she could function almost normally. Her eyes were clearer and her stomach more relaxed from the drink. She took a cold shower, put on some makeup and one of her new outfits, and she looked quite presentable indeed.

The first activity for the congressman's new wife was a charity luncheon where she and the other candidates' wives were the guests of honor. With Dave and Aunt Sussy at her elbows, Gail moved serenely through the sea of bodies, smiling and nodding and offering pleasantries. Aunt Sussy and Dave had given her some last-minute tips. Being a politician's wife was more demanding than being the daughter of one. She had to be very cautious about what she said. But the luncheon passed smoothly. "So far, so good," she told herself when it was all over. "Maybe I'm more suited to this than I thought."

CHAPTER SIX

GAIL WAS IN THE STUDY jotting down notes when Dave and Brad returned to the house. Brad seemed surprisingly cordial as he placed his briefcase on the table beside her and moved to mix drinks for the three of them. He complimented her on her showing at the luncheon and chatted amiably about the afternoon's meeting with Dave.

There was no hint of their encounter the night before; the only thing Gail could detect was a sign of uneasiness in Brad's voice whenever the subject of campaign funds was mentioned. The Harrison camp was still lacking the financial support needed to wage a vigorous fight against Merton Ramsey. As he finished his drink, Brad glanced at his watch. "If you two will excuse me for a while, I've a short errand to run." He rolled down his shirt sleeves and pulled his jacket back on.

As soon as Brad left, Dave walked over to Gail, looking uneasily around the room. "Uh, Gail," he said, reaching into his jacket pocket. "I was going to give you this before you and Brad got married—then I decided it wouldn't be appropriate. But, now well, somehow I think you might need it." He handed her a tiny velvet box. He was obviously embarrassed.

Gail flushed.

"It belonged to my grandmother. It was her good luck charm. She told me to save it for someone special, and you are special, Gail."

Gail opened the box and examined the small gold clover shaped brooch. "Dave, it's lovely. I don't know what to say." She kissed him on the cheek and his hands gently touched her shoulders. "I'd be honored—"

"What the hell is going on?" Brad stormed, as he unexpectedly entered the room.

Gail started to show him the small box but the look of hot anger in his eyes stopped her. She dropped the box into the pocket of her skirt. "Nothing's going on, Brad."

Brad snorted. "You call this little scene *nothing*? I guess I was stupid to throw the two of you together knowing how fond you are of one another, but I never dreamed you would carry on right under my nose." He picked up a sofa pillow and threw it across the room, the force causing a small lamp to topple. "You've had over a week alone— you'd think you could damn well keep your hands off each other until I returned to Washington!"

Dave grabbed his arm. "Brad, you've got it all wrong. I—"

Brad jerked his arm away. "Please don't add insult to injury by demeaning my intelligence. I don't want to hear any so-called explanations. In a couple of hours, we've got to be at that dinner, all pretending this farce of a marriage is the best thing that ever happened." He glared at Gail. "I don't plan that you should lose this election for me, understand?" He took her arm, shoving her toward the stairs. Dave took a step toward Brad, a menacing look in his eyes, but a warning glance from Gail stopped him.

"Brad, you're a damn fool," Dave said.

"Fool is right. But I don't have time for this discussion now—just get out! But be at the hotel later—this isn't over, Dave."

Gail watched from the top of the stairs as Dave walked out of the town house, his clenched fists and taut body giving evidence of his fury.

"Waiting for your lover to leave?" Brad was bounding up the steps, two at a time. Gail turned and ran toward the bedroom, slamming the door and trying to slide the latch in place. But Brad was pushing against the door from the other side. "You may as well let me in! Locks won't keep me out—not for long anyway." She stepped back and his weight sent the door flying open.

He reached roughly around her waist and pulled her to him. "Can't any woman be trusted?"

Something in his tone calmed Gail slightly as she realized Brad's reaction must stem from something deeper than the scene he had just witnessed between her and Dave—much deeper. "It wasn't what it looked like," she said simply.

"Then what was it?" Brad demanded.

She fingered the box in her pocket, unable to show it to Brad and denigrate Dave's offering. "It wasn't anything."

Brad's look changed, from fury to a contemptuous sneer. "I should have known," he growled. "Women are all alike—can't survive a day without a man in their bed. Well, my dear wife, I thought we'd fixed all that. Be assured I'll no longer neglect you." His hands were tangled in her hair and his eyes were icy as he grabbed her face and forced his lips onto hers. She pushed her hands against his chest, jerking her head violently from his. "Brad, no!"

"Brad, yes. You don't tell other men no, my darling wife."

"There are no other men," she protested.

"You mean just Dave?" he sneered. "And when did this, this relationship start?" He pushed her onto the bed, pinning her body under his. "Before our marriage? You two did spend a lot of time together then—didn't you? Dave's an innocent—probably thought about marrying you himself. Little did he know that women always go to the highest bidder. And I've got a lot more money. And status. Haven't I, dear wife?" He made "wife" sound like an obscenity.

Amid the accusations, Brad was trailing his fingertips over her face, her neck, then his hands moved to the buttons of her blouse, deliberately, deftly dissecting each from its buttonhole.

Despite her anger, or perhaps goaded by it, Gail's pulse increased. His lovemaking was a ravishment, an intended punishment, but Gail was so starved for his affection, she found herself succumbing to the whirlpool of passion behind his rage. As though he sensed her surrender, Brad pushed himself away from her. "Why the hell do I even bother with you?" He rose from the bed and withdrew into the bathroom.

Gail lay still for several moments; she heard the water pounding in the shower, the sound only slightly louder than the beating of her heart. She sat up slowly and hung her legs over the side of the bed.

She dressed solemnly, the liveliness of her red chiffon gown camouflaging her somber mood. Silently she put on diamond stud earrings that had belonged to her mother. Gail couldn't bring herself to wear Dave's brooch, not after all that had happened.

As she finished smoothing clear gloss on her swollen lips, she saw Brad in the mirror, standing in the doorway, leaning against the frame. He looked so handsome, his tailored tuxedo molded to his body, and she remembered that first morning in his office. They gazed at each other though the mirror's reflection for a long moment, neither speaking. How could she have felt so angry with him just minutes before and now—now all she could think of was how much she was starting to care for him, in a way she'd never cared for anyone. She was in love with him, as difficult as it was to admit.

A UNIFORMED DOORMAN opened the door of the limousine that had chauffeured them to the Fairmont Hotel. The official purpose of the function was to honor a retiring member of the Louisiana congressional delegation, but an underlying reason for much of the attendance was the chance for Brad to make contacts. The crème de la crème of the Louisiana establishment would be attending the black-tie affair.

As the two climbed from the car, Brad reached for Gail's elbow. He clutched it protectively as they made their way into the hotel lobby. Brad flashed the waiting photographers a mechanical smile, then bent to whisper a reminder to Gail to smile also. His hand sliding from her elbow to the small of her back propelled her past the glaring lights and the approaching reporters. Gail felt certain that Brad's display of husbandly concern served to create the perfect picture of marital bliss Brad desired. Standing near the door of the ballroom was a huge bear of a man at least six foot six and three hundred pounds who Gail instantly recognized as Giles LeBeaux, Cajun businessman, self-made millionaire, with a Cajun accent one could cut with a knife.

"Bonjour, Bradley," he called out, grabbing Brad in a fierce hug.

"Bonjour, Giles," Brad greeted back, his voice muffled by Giles's hug. Brad, a big man himself, appeared almost slight compared to Giles, but then, so did all the other guests.

"And who is this gorgeous creature?" Giles released his hold on Brad and reached for Gail's hand.

A fleeting fear of being squeezed to death passed through Gail's mind as Giles moved closer during Brad's introductions. But instead of a hug, Giles raised her hand to his lips and offered her a gallant kiss.

"My pleasure to meet such a beautiful lady," he murmured. "Bradley, you lucky devil. What did you have to do to get this enchantress to marry you?" Giles seemed oblivious to Brad's lack of response as he placed Gail's hand in the crook of his elbow and led her away to meet the other guests. Brad was left momentarily alone.

"Who's the candidate here anyway?" complained Brad as Tom, the campaign worker, walked up to join him.

"You may have to get used to being upstaged. Your wife has become quite a knockout," Tom replied.

A soft touch at his elbow distracted Brad from the rest of Tom's comments. "Is the congressman being neglected already?" Judith had come up behind him and as he turned around, she planted a quick firm kiss on his lips.

From across the room Gail saw the kiss. She had half a mind to march over and confront Judith but Giles still had her very much in his clutches, and she doubted Brad would appreciate her interference anyway. Gail had been pleased with her appearance tonight, until she caught a glimpse of the glamorous Judith and began comparing herself to the dark-haired beauty. Judith was as dramatic as ever with her jet-black hair and tall, sleek body encased in a slinky gold lamé gown. Gail sighed. How could she ever hope to compete with Judith? She might as well forget her romantic fantasies and get back to the real reason she was married to Brad—to help elect him to the United States Senate—that was all.

The main stumbling block facing Brad's campaign now was the lack of money. If she could only persuade Giles LeBeaux to provide the needed financial support. After all, he was one of the richest men in Louisiana and she did have his attention.

But, try as she might, Gail could not keep the conversation tuned to the campaign. Giles seemed much more interested in paying her an abundance of outrageous compliments as he twirled her around the dance floor. "Madame, you have the mystery of the French woman and the delicate beauty of an English rose. I can tell a volcano exploded in my friend Bradley the moment he saw you. Look at him across the room. He is not happy that I am dominating his wife." Gail looked across the ballroom where Brad stood, Judith DeWitt by his side. If he's as jealous as Giles says, thought Gail, he's certainly keeping it well hidden.

Giles was a surprisingly good dancer for someone of his height and girth, and Gail found herself enjoying the attention she was receiving. It was a totally new experience for her. Yet, she was pleased when she saw Dave approaching; perhaps Dave could help her get Giles back to the topic of campaign financing. But Dave merely greeted Giles warmly and asked if he could cut in. Giles feigned anger, then graciously stepped aside as Dave swept Gail around the dance floor.

"Gail, about this afternoon—"

"I think it's best we forget this afternoon, don't you, Dave? I'm so sorry about what happened. I can't tell you how much your thoughtfulness meant to me. But I can't keep the brooch. I'll have Aunt Sussy return it to you, if that's okay."

"That's fine," he agreed and as though sensing her discomfort, quickly changed the subject.

"Get anywhere with LeBeaux?"

Gail shook her head. "If you mean funding-wise, no. I seem to be striking out totally—perhaps he doesn't like talking business with women," she conceded.

"I don't think that's a problem," Dave assured her. "With your looks and know-how, he couldn't resist you." He smiled down at her. "I'm sure you realize how much we need his support. And I know you can get it, Gail. If anyone can, it's you."

Gail was blushing from Dave's compliments as they left the dance floor. Brad walked over to join them, smiling. When he spoke, there was no evidence of tension in his voice, only a soft seductive quality. "I believe this is our dance, darling," he said, pretending to be charming.

The pretense faded as they moved away from Dave. "I thought I made myself clear this afternoon," he growled in her ear as he pulled her closer to him.

Gail could feel his sinewy thighs pressed against her body and the warmth of his breath sifted through her hair as he spoke. "What are you talking about?" She felt wary—both of her husband and her emotions.

"I'm talking about Dave. Leave it alone." She looked up to see him smiling down at her. His smile would look genuine to onlookers in the ballroom but Gail could sense his controlled resentment, a resentment she couldn't understand. After all, their marriage was simply a charade. She was his wife only because she happened to be available when he needed one. Why should he object to her friendship with Dave? It wasn't as though she meant anything to Brad. Could he actually be jealous?

She continued looking up at him, her eyes glazing like pools of warm brandy. Brad pulled her closer, leading her around the dance floor in silence, as she tried to ignore her strong and ever increasing feelings toward him.

Gail was relieved when the music ended and Brad led her over to a refreshment table where Giles was talking to Dave.

"Bradley," Giles slapped him on the back. "Dave tells me you and your lovely lady are free to join me in Lafayette tomorrow. We'll show Mrs. Harrison a little local *joie de vivre*." Giles turned to Gail, "This weekend we will celebrate in Breaux Bridge and honor the *écrevisse*."

Brad put his arm around Gail's shoulder. "The crawfish—Breaux Bridge is the crawfish capital of the world," he explained. "It's only a few miles from Lafayette."

"And if you've never sampled crawfish, then you're in for a real treat," Dave added.

Gail grimaced involuntarily, evoking a deep belly laugh from Giles. "I'm not sure she's convinced. But I know she'll enjoy the party Angelina and I are having—a true *fais dodo*, with plenty of good Cajun food and music." Giles downed the rest of his drink and set it on the table. "I must be going now. *Au revoir*. Oh, by the way," Giles called over his shoulder as he was leaving, "you and your bride will be my guests of honor."

Brad and Gail smiled in surprise as they turned toward Dave, who was nodding his head in affirmation.

"How did you ever pull that off, you rascal?" Brad slapped Dave on the back in a friendly gesture of approval, then looked at Gail. "You don't know what a coup this is, Gail. Giles LeBeaux is not in the habit of entertaining politicians—his singling us out as his guests of honor can mean only one thing." He laughed as he said the words, "Giles is throwing his political support—and money—into our camp." He patted Dave again. "Good work."

Dave smiled uncomfortably. "You're giving credit to the wrong person, Brad. I'm not the one who delivered—it was Gail."

Gail shook her head in amazement. "But I didn't do anything. The man would hardly let me broach the subject. Or even get a word in edgewise, for that matter. I don't understand him at all."

Brad gave her a puzzled glance, then leaned against the table, his hands pushed inside the pockets of his trousers. "Giles isn't an easy man to understand," Brad began. "He literally grew up roaming the South Louisiana bayous. He's probably on a first-name basis with half the alligators and snakes in those swamps and marshes. It's a tough life and it makes tough men. But at the same time, those Cajun legends and their music seem to add a sort of mellowness to the people. It's hard to explain. It's as if, as these men and women grow up, they come to terms with the elements and discover a special sort of beauty in their environment. They're a unique people. There's no other part of America like Acadiana, Gail. You'll have to understand it a little to understand Giles. And even then, the land—and the people—will still remain a mystery."

Gail listened intently. She could tell Brad loved Louisiana and she wanted to know more about it. "But you said he's a millionaire—how did that happen?"

"Oil," Brad said. "Lafayette used to be a sleepy little village. Then bingo! Offshore petroleum finds and the population zoomed. About one in every forty citizens became a millionaire. It turned into something like a miniature Kuwait."

"It should prove to be an interesting weekend," Gail smiled.

"That it should," Brad agreed.

GAIL WATCHED Brad as he circled in front of the car after helping her inside. Her husband was becoming more of an enigma each day. She was certain when Sam had persuaded her to work for Brad that she had him pegged right—a shallow, socialite playboy who wanted to make a name for himself in politics. But the more she came to know Brad, the less she felt she knew him. She gazed down at the rings he'd given her on their wedding night. They were a reminder he did pay a lot of attention to detail. He left nothing to chance. Just as with his work. She'd discovered Brad wrote all of his speeches himself or, if necessary, he simply spoke off-the-cuff. His knowledge of the environment was endless. He knew every facet, every fact, and he certainly understood how to work a crowd, whether it be a gathering of wealthy establishment types like the evening before, or a group of blue-collar workers at a glove factory. She smiled as she thought of their first early-morning session in the rain.

She turned to look at Brad, his hands placed casually on the steering wheel as they headed west on the highway. He was in complete control of the powerful automobile, just as he seemed to be in control of every part of his life. Except for his relationship with his wife. Gail was still puzzled over his behavior the evening before. She gazed out her window.

She, Brad, Dave and several campaign workers had spent several hours after the gala drinking café au lait and eating powdered-sugar *beignets* as they discussed Giles LeBeaux. Gail had never seen Dave so effusive, giving Gail full credit for LeBeaux's invitation. The others responded with lavish compliments.

Her husband, to her dismay, wasn't as charitable. Gail couldn't help noticing that while Brad was being uncharacteristically charming and attentive to her, he avoided joining in the group's enthusiastic praise. It really didn't matter—what was important was that they now might have the financial support to wage an effective battle against Ramsey.

Gail had enjoyed herself, chatting until the wee hours of morning. It was a far cry from the earlier events of the day. Even Brad seemed relaxed, carefree.

So, she had been totally unprepared for his attack when they returned to the town house. "Well, did I play my role well, Mrs. Harrison?" he asked sardonically. "Was I convincing as the adoring husband?" Gail stared at him in wonderment as he closed the door behind them and began loosening his tie. Now what was the matter? What had she done this time? she asked herself.

"Of course," she said, replying in kind. "You're always convincing when there's a crowd. Ever the competent politician."

"That sharp tongue of yours will be your undoing," he snarled as he wrapped his fingers around her arm. Gail tensed as she felt the bruising pressure. This was crazy. He'd seemed so happy as they bade the others good-night only minutes before. Now he was absolutely livid. Over what?

"What's going on with you?" she demanded.

"Don't play dumb." He gave her a piercing stare. "Just you remember you have a husband now. So don't let all the male attention you were reveling in tonight go to your head. If it requires a chastity belt and a padlock on the door, dear wife, that's what you'll get. You'll be in no other man's bed!"

Gail's body shook in indignation as his message sank in. "Well, since it's not likely I'll be in yours again either, perhaps I'd better consider a hot-water bottle or an electric blanket for winter. Fortunately, it's too warm for either tonight." She jerked out of his grasp and stormed up the stairs shutting herself in her room. She feared another confrontation, more uncalled-for hostility, but Brad went quietly to the guest bedroom, and they spent another night as they spent most nights—apart.

Gail glanced across the front seat at Brad again. His gaze was straight ahead, glued to the road. She wished she could figure out what he was thinking, feeling—what was going on behind those eyes. If only she were more intuitive, then perhaps she could understand this man she'd married. Why had he been so agitated the evening before? Jealousy couldn't explain it away completely, she decided. But possessiveness might. He probably thought "What's mine is mine, even if I don't want it." She involuntarily rubbed the faint bruises which had appeared on her upper arm as a result of his rough grasp, and was glad she'd had the foresight to wear a long-sleeved dress.

They'd been driving over a bridge for ages. It had to be the longest one Gail had ever seen. "The Atchafalaya Swamp," Brad commented, as though reading her mind. She was startled he'd finally spoken and was hopeful she might use this as a starting point for further conversation, but he said nothing more. Apparently, he'd decided talking to his wife was not worth the effort unless there was an audience around. So the two continued their trip in silence.

There was no silence once they arrived at Giles LeBeaux's mansion, though. He had advised Gail he had a large family, but large was an understatement, and she was quite taken aback as the introductions began. There was his wife, Angelina, and his eight children, plus numerous sisters, brothers, in-laws, cousins. To an only child like Gail, it was an overwhelming experience.

Anyone inclined to think of Giles as a bumbling backwoodsman who'd happened to strike it rich, would have abandoned those thoughts observing his skill in managing the afternoon. After lunch, a group had sequestered itself in Giles's office. There was Giles, Gail, Brad, Dave, plus a small group of local businessmen.

Gail was the only woman in the group, and she was surprised she'd been included. She'd expected to be relegated to the kitchen, with the other women, to help prepare for the evening festivities.

Despite Dave's compliments of the evening before, Gail still wasn't convinced she had anything to do with Giles's decision to support Brad. The only conclusion she could possibly draw was that Giles had already made his decision and had simply picked last evening to advise the Harrison camp. One thing was sure, she thought ruefully, whatever the reason, her part in it would fail to please Brad.

Either way, he would find something at fault with her. Oh well, she decided as she glanced about the small room, she wasn't about to question her good fortune at being included. Even if her husband didn't realize the value of her contribution to the campaign, at least it was gratifying to know others recognized her input.

Giles got straight to the point. He informed Brad he was throwing his support behind the Harrison campaign. He would host a major fund-raiser in New Orleans or Baton Rouge within a month or so. The bargain was sealed with handshakes.

With financial worries relieved, the campaign could proceed in earnest—with a focus on issues and the merits of the candidates. For three hours a strategy session ensued as the room filled with smoke from cigars and heat from disagreements over approaches. Finally Giles called a halt to the proceedings. "Enough," he declared in a booming voice, standing up to make his point. "It's time to get ready for the celebration. We can argue later."

Brad rose and stood next to Gail, resting his hand on her shoulders and gently massaging her neck with his fingers. The gesture was relaxing, yet disturbing. She felt the hairs on her neck stand up and she even shuddered slightly as Brad's voice murmured in her ear, "Why don't we take a little nap before the party?" Brad's voice was just loud enough for the others in the room to hear. There was a snicker or two and one of the men winked knowingly at Brad. Gail blushed, her cheeks turning a bright crimson, but she managed to hold her tongue and play the dutiful bride.

A nap was exactly what Brad meant. They'd no sooner made their way to their appointed guest room than he flopped down on the king-size bed, apparently exhausted. Gail watched in amazement as he lay motionless then quickly fell into a deep sleep. Resignedly, she unpacked and took her toiletries into the bathroom. While Brad was sleeping, she enjoyed a long relaxing soak. The effect was pure magic—the warmth of the water soothed her taut nerves and calmed her spirits. After drying off, she put on a cotton bathrobe and lay down on the other side of the bed. Soon she was sleeping also.

ONE SIMPLY had to experience a *fais dodo* to understand it, Gail decided, for it defied description. Lively, sometimes haunting, music filled the evening air. Tables were laden with regional foods—pots of jambalaya and pungent gumbos, mounds of rusty-red crawfish, crumbly sugar cakes.

Whole families came together. Children, unobserved by parents, feasted on powdery sweet confections. Babies nestled in mothers' and grandmothers' arms. Young and old were eating, dancing and chattering in their unique French, adhering to the customs and culture that had been identified with their area of the United States for almost two centuries.

Gail learned that the word *Cajun* came from the term Acadian. Before the American Revolution, their French ancestors had come to this wild, bayou-streaked land from present-day Nova Scotia, a province in Eastern Canada. They had been expelled from the country for refusing to forsake their Roman Catholic religion and give allegiance to the English King. Only a few thousand survived the brutal Le Grande Derangement that transported them south to this vast wilderness. Gail remembered the plight of the refugees as immortalized in Longfellow's "Evangeline." She vowed to become reacquainted with the poem now that she'd experienced the land and its people firsthand.

"Having a good time?" Brad touched her arm as he spoke.

"Matter of fact, I am. It's like a living history lesson. And Giles is an excellent host." She moved a few steps away from Brad.

He strolled after her, now seemingly interested in conversation. "Not too many people outside Louisiana realize what kinds of contrasts exist within this state." He sighed. "I love it, couldn't think of living anywhere else." He again took her arm, more firmly this time, holding Gail in place. She couldn't escape his grasp, not unless she wanted to cause a scene. What was Brad trying to do to her, anyway?

There were no speeches that evening; on the surface it was purely a social affair. Yet Giles took pains to introduce the Harrisons to all of the guests and Gail felt sure many of them would be contributing to the campaign coffers. She was weary and grateful, when the evening finally came to a close, and she and Brad could say good-night to their host and hostess.

CHAPTER SEVEN

GAIL KICKED off her shoes and perched on the edge of the bed, reaching down to massage her feet. She'd been standing for the better part of the evening.

"Feet tired? I'm not surprised. They're so tiny and delicate." Brad stooped and took one foot in his hand. He started massaging it tenderly. It was a soothing, almost sensual experience for Gail as Brad continued his firm stroking. She was leaning back on her arms and had to resist reaching out to touch him. She couldn't bear his rejection. Not again. Even though she wasn't sure from the tender look in his eyes that he would reject her this time, she dared not risk exposing her feelings.

Brad appeared reluctant to break the contact. He started to speak but instead carefully returned her foot to the floor, gave it a little pat, massaged the other one briefly and walked into the bathroom. The close quarters of the room seemed even closer to Gail. There was no place to hide and she didn't know what to expect next from Brad. But he was quite casual when he returned. "Want a glass of water or anything before we go to bed?"

"No, thank you."

"Fine. See you in the morning then." He pulled down the covers and got into bed—turning his back to Gail.

Brad had apparently declared a marital truce as he was totally charming the next morning. They had a quick breakfast with Giles and Angelina and bid them warm thanks and goodbye. In the car Brad talked of his plans for the next few months. He would return to Washington the next day, but today he and Gail would play tourist and see more of Acadiana before returning to the plantation.

They toured the Acadian Village Museum and Gardens. Gail felt as if she'd stepped into the past as they walked among the cabins clustered beside a man-made bayou. They drove south to St. Martinville and strolled beneath the "Evangeline Oak" where Longfellow's lovers were reunited, then stopped for cups of thick, black coffee. As dusk approached, they drove to Greenbriar, again in silence. This time, however, the silence was comfortable; it had been a lovely day, surprisingly free of tension.

But they'd no sooner stepped in the door of Brad's antebellum home than the tranquility was broken. "I'd like to speak to you in the den for a few minutes before I go."

"You're leaving now?"

"I'll spend the night at the town house in New Orleans so I can catch an early flight back to D.C. But we need to get one thing straight before I leave. You are to remain here in residence while I'm away." Again there was a flickering in the depths of Brad's eyes—that elusive something that Gail sensed more than saw as he handed out his orders.

Gail hadn't been prepared for Brad's announcement. She stood in place, stunned as Brad moved around the desk and sat down, leaning back comfortably. She felt as if she were standing in reprimand before him, a child before a scolding parent. She didn't like this position of power he had assumed. Especially since she knew only too well his power over her wasn't an assumption—it was real. Brad Harrison was in control of her, body and soul. She didn't like it one bit, and she'd be darned if she'd let it show. She had to tough it out, to meet him eye to eye. She reached back and felt for the chair before sitting down.

"I can't believe what you're saying, Brad. I thought the whole purpose of this—this marriage was so I could be the dutiful wife out campaigning with you—help you gain a new positive image. A constant Harrison presence in the state. I acceded to your request that I keep a low profile after the marriage and honeymoon, and perhaps it was useful—the mystery bit and all. But I really question the judgment of my hiding away at the plantation when I should be out meeting the voters."

"Gail, I'm making you the executive campaign consultant, and you need to be where Evelyn can easily locate you in case she runs into trouble. Evelyn's eager and willing but she hasn't had a great deal of experience in managing a campaign and she might have to call on you. I need Dave free to come and go, though I expect him to spend most of his time in Washington." He folded his hands behind his head and leaned back farther, propping a loafered foot on the desk.

"But I still don't understand. What good can I be here at the plantation? If Evelyn needs assistance, I should be at campaign headquarters."

"Nonsense. You can get a lot more done here, without outside distractions. And I hope you'll do a lot of good. You were the Louisiana campaign manager, right? This is a logical promotion, right? You do have the confidence of the party machinery, right? You delivered Giles LeBeaux, right?" He sat up and propped his arms on the desk as he hammered away. Gail was becoming angrier by the moment. She hated the way he was punctuating the end of his sentences... She was tired of hearing, "right." She knew only too well the innuendo behind those little stabs. He wasn't asking, he was telling.

Brad was supposedly putting her back in charge of the Louisiana campaign office, but she was to operate undercover, out at the plantation. She wasn't to set foot in the state campaign headquarters or on the campaign trail unless she was on his arm. Executive campaign consultant—it was just a meaningless title thrust at her so she wouldn't complain. The truth of the matter was that Brad was trying to put her on ice at the plantation. But why? What possible value could she be to him just sitting around waiting for him to return?

"Well?" He was leaning forward on the desk. "Do you agree?"

"And if I don't? I get the impression you're giving me little choice in the matter."

"I always knew you were bright, Gail," he said sarcastically. "You will assume this new title and you will remain here until I return." He smiled a cold, satisfied smile.

"So all you want me to do is sit here and twiddle my thumbs until you return to take me, the dutiful wife, out of the closet and go campaigning. You couldn't care less about my skills, my expertise."

His smile warmed; she almost felt he was laughing at her. "It's comforting you're beginning to understand. We just might make a success of this marriage after all."

"Marriage? Don't you mean mockery? Fat chance of it ever being successful—unless you gauge success only with capturing a Senate seat!"

He was around the desk in a flash, grasping her wrist and pulling her from the chair. Gail was too astounded to protest when his lips crushed hers, unleashing the emotion that had been boiling within him. Her first sensation was a feeling of entrapment, then her senses began swirling to his touch, her anger melting into passion at the feel of his tongue parting her lips, as though she were drowning in a vortex of longing.

Brad's demanding kiss became tender as he gently claimed her lips. His hands caressed her upperarms, her back, and she responded in kind, letting her fingers trace the hairline at the back of his neck and move on to his straight, muscled spine. Gail could feel the rapid beating of his heart and knew her own heartbeat was keeping pace with his.

Then suddenly he released her, his eyes smoky as he stared into her own. She thought she saw reluctance in his blue depths as she returned his gaze evenly. But his expression changed, hardened. "Something to remember me by," he said sardonically, "while you're working out here." He turned toward the door and in an instant he was gone. Gail stared at the door. She had half a mind to chase him up the stairs and slap his arrogant face. But that would mean she was playing his own crazy game. Besides it would give him too much satisfaction. No, she would just count to ten and compose herself. She was already at a hundred when the door opened.

"Well, well," twittered Aunt Sussy as she encountered Gail. "Bradley just said goodbye. Tell me what happened? Did you have a successful weekend?"

Gail put down the campaign material she was pretending to read. "Aunt Sussy, I'm glad you're back here. Yes, and I don't know. If you mean was it successful politically—yes. If you mean is the marriage successful...I can't answer that. The time we spent together was pleasant," she said. Some of it, she thought ruefully. No use burdening Aunt Sussy with her problems.

"Well—I never did ask you what my nephew thought of your new look?" Aunt Sussy was pouring the tea she'd carried in on a tray.

"He didn't seem to think much about it."

"Oh, Bradley thought about it all right."

"Well, he sure kept his thoughts to himself. It makes me wonder what's the use. I'll never be the kind of woman he wants—voluptuous, empty-headed, subservient."

"For someone he doesn't care for, he certainly spends a lot of time with you."

"Just for show. Remember this is a . . . oh, Aunt Sussy, it sounds like a soap opera! This is a marriage of convenience. When it isn't convenient anymore, it'll be over." She took a sip of her tea. "Guess what my instructions are? I'm to sit here at the plantation and wait for my lord and master to return. Isn't that a laugh?"

Aunt Sussy gazed at her, silently, apparently unable to offer consolation. "Well, what are you going to do, dear?"

"I'm going to get that nephew of yours elected to the Senate. And I'm going to do it by working—not by sitting."

"Good for you," Aunt Sussy said. She patted Gail's hand. "Good for you."

"But I thought you were exiled to the plantation." Dave's grin indicated that he considered Brad's instructions as ludicrous as Gail did.

"I was." Gail sat down in the chair across from Dave's desk. "Actually I tried staying there for a few days, just so I could tell Brad I gave his 'suggestion' a fair trial. I slept late, read the newspaper from front page to classifieds, took long walks around the plantation grounds and swam thirty laps in the pool every afternoon. Then I decided I'd had enough. I was desperate for work again. It was either work on the campaign and upset Brad, or run the plantation—and get the manager in a huff."

Gail ran her fingers through her hair. "I have to tell you the plantation manager wasn't too keen on having me underfoot. He snarled every time I asked a question and all I could get out of him was a speedy tour through the sugar cane fields in his Jeep, and he did it grudgingly at that. So I decided to work on the campaign—Brad seemed the lesser of the two evils."

"Well, I've missed you," Dave said. "I tried to get news about you through Sam. But the old reprobate is on a junket to some agricultural sites in South America. At least I get to see you before I leave."

"Oh no, you're leaving now?"

"I'm off to D.C. tomorrow for about a week. It's nice you'll be here to help Evelyn out."

"Did I hear my name being taken in vain?" Evelyn popped into the room. "Gail! What are you doing here? Brad said you'd be working out of the plantation."

"Brad must learn that he doesn't always get his way. I can't laze about at Greenbriar when there's so much real work to be done here."

Evelyn and Dave exchanged knowing glances. "Looks like the campaign is going to be even more exciting than we thought," she said. "Brad usually does get his way."

"Then it's time for a change," Gail retorted. "Besides, an exciting campaign will be better than a losing one. Now let's get to work."

The next few weeks flew by for Gail, even though she missed Brad and longed to hear from him. He called campaign headquarters daily, but he wasn't aware Gail was there. No one volunteered the information. Especially not Gail, who thought it best not to make an issue by telephone of her decision to return to New Orleans and active campaigning. They could hash it out when he came back to Louisiana. Maybe by that time he'd see she had made the right decision, that she needed to be at the center of the action. On Saturday, she and Aunt Sussy lunched together at the town house. Aunt Sussy was leaving the next day to visit her sister in Monroe. "Gail, your metamorphosis is complete. Your new look and the work you've been doing—well it just all agrees with you. I can't wait for Bradley to return."

Gail missed Brad and wanted him to come home to her even though she was slightly fearful of how he'd react to her having defied his orders. Even if theirs was an imperfect—to say the least—relationship, she still had faint hopes of forging out a marriage. Apparently Brad hadn't even tried to contact her since his return to Washington. Aunt Sussy or Calvin would have told her if he'd called. Brad would have surely tracked her down at the town house, especially if he'd called the plantation and found her gone. She should have been happy he hadn't discovered that she'd left Greenbriar but some days she had wished for a call even though she knew Brad would be furious with her. At least she would have received some attention. The truth of it, she admitted sadly, was that she simply mattered so little to him that she was not even worth the trouble of a telephone call.

Oh, well, she consoled herself, there was nothing she could do to change that, but she could take advantage of her afternoon off. She changed into a swimsuit and grabbed a bottle of suntan lotion. With any luck there was time to catch an hour of sun on the town house patio before she had to dress for the committee meeting that night.

Gail spread the bright-colored beach towel on the flagstone patio and stretched out. The Louisiana sun had tanned her skin to a soft bronze, making her hair seem blonder and her eyes glow brighter. She laughed and thought ironically that marriage to Brad Harrison had been the best diet she'd ever been on—perhaps she should write a book about it. Effective diet remedies always sold well. Watching her weight used to be one of her major priorities. Now, she barely thought about food—or eating. She'd lost almost ten pounds since her marriage and her petite frame had become softly-angled. Simply put, Gail had become a beautiful woman with a stunning figure.

BRAD HADN'T RETURNED to Louisiana when Gail expected. She'd heard by way of Evelyn that he had remained for several crucial meetings and wasn't sure when he'd be able to get back. The only contact Gail had had with Brad in the past few weeks was watching him on the evening news. Dave and the public relations people in Washington were doing a good job. Brad had appeared on several weekly news interview programs and had made all the network morning talk shows. Even though he wasn't in Louisiana personally, his message was getting through.

Gail felt sure she would collapse if she had to endure one more tea party or luncheon. Her feet were swollen from all the standing around in high heels and her head hurt from the forced conversation and constant smiling. It was Friday morning and she didn't feel a bit more rested than she had when she had gone to bed the night before. The thought of going to work made her groan. She sat on the edge of the bed with her head in her hands.

"I know what I need," she said to herself. "I need a break." She checked her datebook—no appointments today. "That settles it. I'm going to play hooky, then head to the plantation for the weekend. I'm beginning to miss the place." She grabbed the phone for a quick call to Evelyn.

Gail was singing in enjoyment as the sleek sports car she drove purred along the interstate headed toward Greenbriar. She had gone back to bed and slept until ten, then shopped, had a relaxing lunch and picked up a couple of paperbacks. She would be at the plantation in time for the six o'clock news. Her day had been wonderfully relaxing, exactly what she had needed, she thought as she parked the car in the circular drive, pulling her parcels from the seat beside her. It had been such a treat to escape from work for a day—as much as she loved it. Her hand had just touched the doorknob when the door flew open.

"Where the hell have you been?" A scowling Brad confronted her.

She might have known he'd pick this day to return. "New Orleans," she replied casually, walking past him into the house and placing her packages on a Victorian settee.

"You weren't at campaign headquarters—I know because I've been there all day." His face was flushed.

"No, not at campaign headquarters. Today was a play day." She kicked off her shoes and walked into the den, strolling over to the bar and chunking a couple of ice cubes into a glass. She wasn't going to let him ruffle her.

Brad was after her in a flash. "Who did you spend the day with?"

"My favorite person." Gail tossed him an enigmatic look and pulled a bottle of soda from the bar refrigerator.

Brad circled the bar and stood hovering over her. "I'm not in the mood for games. Talk. And I mean now. Who did you spend the day with? It was Dave, wasn't it? That's who you were with. I knew he really wasn't going out to see his mother."

Gail coolly moved away from him and opened the bottle. She was enjoying his discomfort. Served him right for trying to bully her. She poured the soda into her glass. "I haven't seen Dave today. As I said, I spent the day with my favorite person—me. Now, if you want a minute-by-minute report, the credit card receipts in my purse can probably provide it." She gestured toward the foyer. "I bought two shirts, a pair of slacks, a couple of dresses, three paperbacks, and had lunch at Gallatoire's. The evidence is over there in the shopping bags. Except for the lunch, of course." She smiled up at him. He looked perplexed, even sheepish.

She felt oddly satisfied being on top in an encounter with Brad. Too often he was in control, the one pulling the strings. Gail was proud she'd handled this situation so calmly and adeptly. She strolled over to the couch and collapsed, propping her feet up. Brad stayed behind the bar, watching her as he poured himself a cola. A few minutes later he had joined her on the couch.

"I understand you've been doing a great job on the campaign."

"Oh? What do you mean?"

"Don't play dumb. I was only at the office for fifteen minutes before I spotted that rabbit paperweight of yours. And what do you know—next to it was a draft of a press release in your handwriting. Under duress, Evelyn admitted you'd been working there, and she also let me know how grateful she'd been that you were."

Gail was surprised at his tone. He sounded almost contrite. She remembered their parting, the anger mixed with passion. Something in their relationship must have changed. Brad seemed calmer, more reasonable. She wasn't sure what to think of him now anymore than she knew what to think of him then. She didn't understand the man. All she knew was that she loved him. Yes. She loved him. But she wasn't sure he could be trusted—not yet. His hot-and-cold ways were too fresh in her mind.

Just what was he up to, though? He reached over and trailed a finger down her cheek, a simple, yet titillating gesture. Gail longed for him to take her in his arms, to quiet her fears. She wanted this to be a real marriage, even though it had started off as a temporary arrangement. Their time together had altered the agreement, had created feelings that hadn't existed before. Feelings of love . . . at least on her part.

She wanted his lips to touch hers . . . she waited still and silent as he watched her. Then he spoke, breaking the spell. "I'll be around for the next week or so. I've a whole slew of campaign appearances lined up. But I'd like to ask you a favor."

Gail was thrilled. She could hardly believe her ears. Was he actually pleased with her work on the campaign? No. All Brad wanted from her was to have a dinner party at the plantation. A sit-down dinner for a dozen or so guests, then a larger reception afterward for about a hundred people. He wanted her to tend to the details.

He reached into his pocket and pulled out a folded sheet of paper. "The guest list. If you should think of anyone else, I'm sure we could squeeze in a few more."

She unfolded the paper and scanned the list. "No, this looks fine. Is there a special meal you'd like. Or shall I just take care of it?"

"No, I'm sure whatever you serve will be perfect. The only problem is time. I've been rather presumptuous—we sent out invitations from D.C. for Saturday night. We could get Aunt Sussy back from Monroe if you need her. Of course, Crystal's a gem, and you can always call Judith. She's had lots of experience with this sort of thing."

Gail froze at the mention of Judith DeWitt. Brad might believe his wife had limited political skills. But was he now implying she had no social ones, that she couldn't even arrange a simple party. "I'll call someone if I need help," she mumbled irritably.

What's the matter with me, Gail wondered. She'd been assured Brad and Judith were simply old friends, political allies. But she couldn't help worrying about Judith. It wasn't simply that the woman was so beautiful. She was also a part of Brad's world—a world of plantation houses and debutante balls, of gracious living and family ties stretching back for generations. It was so different from the rural life in southeastern Oklahoma Gail had known as a young child. Here, everything was tradition. Gail felt like an outsider in Brad's world.

Being a senator's daughter and living in Washington had exposed her to wealth and elegance, but power in the nation's capital turned on an election result. It wasn't who your family was that mattered, but how many terms you'd served and what kind of committees you sat on. For the nonelected, there was another structure—who were you married to, or whose staff were you on. Naturally, those associated with the White House carried the most prestige.

Gail asked herself for the thousandth time why Brad hadn't married Judith; they certainly seemed to enjoy each other. She fit in to his sphere so well, was to the manor born, so to speak. The only explanation had to be that he thought marriage to a divorced woman might hurt his political image. After all, his whole life centered on politics. Gail's had also, but she was beginning to realize it might not be such a healthy lifestyle. There was so much else to learn about. Perhaps she should think of something different to do, a new career, when Brad's campaign was over.

Brad stayed at the plantation only long enough to discuss the party, then he was off again, a pat on the arm the extent of his husbandly affection. Gail saw him again later in the week with Dave, but mostly she followed his whereabouts by way of the newspapers and television. He was campaigning vigorously throughout the state. So much for new beginnings.

She sat at her desk sipping her morning coffee and charting the results of the latest polls. Things were definitely improving. She glanced up at the portable television droning away in the corner and saw Brad—on a talk show out of Baton Rouge. As usual, he was smiling his toothy political smile and charming the show's hostess to the point where she could barely remember her questions. Gail's name came up often in the interview, and Gail decided Brad was performing a bit too much like the adoring husband. She'd have to remind him when he came home not to overplay his part.

Gail watched her husband intently. He was undoubtedly the most attractive man she'd ever seen. She thought of being in his arms and of him telling her that he loved her, that he'd always loved her. And then he'd compliment her on her intelligence and political acumen. *Silly*, thought Gail, *Brad will never think of me like that. I'm only married to him because I happen to have been in the right place—or was that the wrong place—at the right time?*

Gail returned to the plantation on Friday after doing some shopping in town, but Brad didn't make it home that night as she had expected. About ten she received a call from Evelyn saying that he was still involved in strategy sessions and had decided to spend the night in New Orleans. He'd be back at the plantation the next afternoon in plenty of time for the party. Gail was disappointed Brad hadn't phoned himself. Was she just another detail for the campaign machinery to take care of? She went into the kitchen and opened the warmer to remove the dinner Crystal had saved for Brad. After simmering for hours, it had shriveled to an unappetizing lump. Gail raked it into the garbage disposal and placed the plate in the dishwasher. Then she climbed up the stairs to her bedroom to spend another night alone.

Saturday rushed by. At five o'clock Gail made a final inspection of the dining room. The mahogany table had been extended to serve sixteen people. Through the windows of the dining room, Gail could see the workmen decorating the patio and lawn for the party which would follow dinner.

Gail smiled in satisfaction as her eyes turned back to the lovely room. A Waterford crystal chandelier hung regally over the gleaming table which was already set with Harrison family silver and china. Crystal goblets sat waiting to be filled with the wines Gail had selected. A shining silver candelabra with creamy-white tapers surrounded by an elaborate arrangement of pastel blossoms formed the centerpiece. Hand-embroidered white linen place mats and napkins matched the needlepoint cushions of the chairs. The room was perfect. Brad would have to be impressed.

Gail glanced at her watch. The first guests would be arriving in little more than an hour and still she hadn't heard from Brad. She was upset at his tardiness but decided she'd better get dressed so at least one of the Harrisons would be on hand to greet their guests.

She had just removed her clothing and was already entering the bathroom when she saw him. Gail emitted a little gasp as she took in Brad reclining in the oval-shaped tub, apparently asleep. Her eyes wandered from his toes upward over his body; she was embarrassed when she got to Brad's eyes to discover them open, a big grin on his face. His eyes turned serious as they started their own survey. Gail had forgotten she, too, was nude. She reached for a towel as his laugh vibrated through the small room. "Don't be so modest, Gail. Come join me." His hand snaked out to pull her, sputtering, into the tub with him.

Gail opened her mouth for a token protest, but was silenced by Brad's lips. Her own lips parted in anticipation as he savored the hollows of her mouth, their tongues meeting in warm hunger.

A hard rapping on the bedroom door disturbed their lovemaking. Brad pulled away from her. "Don't go away," he cautioned as he wrapped a towel around his torso.

In a few moments he was back. "Our guests are already arriving. I'll get dressed quickly—and reluctantly—and join them." He smiled and bent over the tub to kiss the tip of Gail's nose. "Later," he promised.

When Gail returned to the bedroom wrapped in a fluffy bath towel, Brad was already in his tuxedo. "I didn't know what you planned to wear tonight," he told her as he took a long black velvet box from the dresser top. "But I hope these match your outfit."

Gail opened the box and saw a rainbow of gems. A necklace of mixed stones—sapphire, topaz, tourmaline, peridot, garnet, and amethyst set in gold, with matching earrings. It was as though Brad had a sixth sense; they would be perfect with the dress she'd planned to wear. She lifted her eyes to meet his. "They're very lovely. I don't know what to say. Thank you, Brad."

He kissed her again lightly, then left to join their company. Her head was swimming as she sat on the bed, fingering the jewelry. What was happening here tonight, to her and Brad? Brad was treating her the way she'd always fantasized he would. Was she destined to wake up in a few moments and discover she had dreamed it all? Dream or not—Gail was ecstatic.

She felt like Scarlett O'Hara descending the staircase at Tara. Brad was in the foyer with Giles LeBeaux and two other men and they all watched her as she made her entrance. She nervously smoothed the creamy beige taffeta of her ballgown as she came down the steps slowly. The dress was bare-shouldered, the bodice narrowing at her tiny waist and the skirt flaring fully all the way to her ankles. She wore Brad's gift, the loveliness of the jewels merely accenting her own beauty.

After greeting everyone and sipping cocktails for an hour, Brad and Gail led the group to the dining room. The tiny, dancing flames of the candles seemed to reflect the intimate but lively tone the evening embraced. Gail had decided to follow the old Creole tradition and serve three courses. The first course was a salad of fresh vegetables— cold radishes, celery and cucumbers and firm, tiny tomatoes. Next the waiters served roasted oysters with small new potatoes, then filets of veal and steamed green beans followed by an airy raspberry Bavarian cream. French wines had been served throughout the meal—a possible political *faux pas* in any other part of the United States, but not in southern Louisiana.

After dinner they retired to the parlor for coffee and liqueurs and awaited the arrival of the rest of the guests. Her dinner a success, Gail sat back contentedly and watched the group as Calvin served them cups of rich café au lait. She felt confident Brad had been pleased with the dinner; she only hoped the remainder of the evening would go as smoothly, that the bubble wouldn't pop.

When the party was finally winding down hours later, she was wondering why she'd been so apprehensive. It had been a gala evening; the guests all laughing, talking and mingling. A society columnist from New Orleans had interviewed Gail, and Brad joined her just in time to provide a twosome for the newspaper's photographer.

It appeared there would be good press—precisely what the campaign needed. Brad had received a lot of coverage that week. On Wednesday, he'd been pictured chatting with factory workers in a cafeteria. On Thursday, he was photographed bending over to admire a fisherman's catch at Black Lake. This coverage would round things out perfectly, making Brad look like a man who fit in anywhere, a man for all the people.

Judith wasn't at the party, and Gail chastised herself for her feelings of relief. After all, Brad didn't include Judith in everything. If the earlier events of the evening meant anything, it appeared Gail had little to be worried about. She seemed to have finally got the man's attention. She didn't need to worry about Judith or any other woman, for that matter.

Giles had claimed her for several dances; his wife protesting that she was feeling neglected, but Angelina had said it with a teasing laugh. It was evident they were very much in love, after all those years of marriage, and all those children. Gail suddenly felt a wave of depression. She knew that was how she wanted Brad to feel about her, but it had seemed hopeless. Or was it? He was beginning to desire her, the scene in the bathtub left no doubt about that. He had given her this lovely present; her hands went up to finger the necklace around her throat. But desire wasn't love. And presents, this present, could simply be part of the act. After all, the jewelry would stand out in the news photograph and serve to reinforce the myth of the happy and successful couple.

Gail was checking the refreshment table when Brad came up behind her, putting his arm around her and kissing her on the neck. "You haven't danced with me all evening." It sounded like an accusation.

"You haven't asked me," Gail retorted.

"Well, I'll remedy that right now. Dance with me, Mrs. Harrison," he whispered into her ear.

Her senses flamed when he took her in his arms and pressed his body close to hers. She closed her eyes and no longer heard the chatter of their guests, or even the music playing, for Brad was her whole world at that moment. He'd whisked her to a place she'd never been: a place only for lovers, a place with no beginning, no end—only Brad, holding her, always. A sweet reality crept in as she opened her eyes. They were still dancing, but now were alone, in the rose garden. His lips were covering hers and she was in ecstasy. She wished the dance would never stop, that this moment would go on forever.

THEIR GUESTS had all departed by midnight; except for the few who were staying over. Brad and Giles were secluded in his study both smoking fat cigars when Gail went in to say good-night. Brad's look gave her no doubt he would soon be joining her.

Gail pulled her filmiest negligee from a hanger and threw it across the bed. She undressed quickly, removing her gown and hanging it carefully. She examined herself in the full-length mirror, nude save for the jewelry she was still wearing. She traced her hand over her body, pleased. She now liked her body, and felt no trace of her old insecurities as she wondered whether Brad could love her and be as proud of her as she wanted him to be. Gail reached up and took off her earrings and unfastened the clasp of the necklace. She pulled the soft, silver-white negligee over her head and sat at the dressing table, brushing her hair until it shone.

Thirty minutes had passed and Brad still hadn't joined her. Restless, Gail strolled over to the window. There was a full moon shining, illuminating the couple embracing on the driveway. Must be stragglers, Gail thought. She smiled wistfully until she suddenly realized who she was seeing—unmistakably, it was Brad with Judith. Tears came to Gail's eyes but they didn't blind her to the stunning woman gazing into her husband's eyes. Judith was laughing as she got into the car and drove away. Gail couldn't see the look on Brad's face.

She hadn't had time to dress when he joined her moments later, only time to pull off the negligee. She was standing there naked when Brad closed the door behind him.

"Are you in that much of a hurry?" he teased.

"For you, hardly!" Gail snapped. She walked over to the closet.

"It seems you've worked yourself into a temper. I shouldn't have kept you waiting so long." He smiled as he removed his bow tie and unbuttoned the top button of his shirt.

Gail was pulling on a robe.

"That's not necessary. You're just going to take it off again." Brad seemed to ignore her anger. He sat on the edge of the bed and continued to disrobe, now removing his shoes and socks.

Gail was muttering as she struggled with the belt of her robe, which was twisted into a knot.

Brad got up. "What's with you?" He moved his arms inside the robe and pressed against her.

"Leave me alone!" Gail demanded. She tried to push him away.

"No. No, I don't plan to leave you alone. Not any longer. And I really don't think you want me to." He stared down at her. "Why have you done such an about-face since the rose garden?" Then his eyes lit up. "You saw Judith, didn't you? That little demon jealousy has caused your change of mood." He chuckled as he tightened his grip on her.

"I'm not jealous. Just leave me alone." Her frustration was mounting as she tried futilely to get out of his embrace.

"Hey, that's not good for my ego." He was still grinning, obviously relishing the situation.

His casual manner made her even madder. "Get someone else to flatter your ego, if that's what you need. I'm not the type to gaze up into your eyes and giggle at your stupid jokes."

Brad said nothing.

"Don't ignore me," she stammered.

"I don't plan to," he reached up and eased the robe off her shoulder.

"Stop that." She pulled the robe back up. "Why did you agree to marry me, Brad? Why didn't you marry Judith?"

"Perhaps Judith didn't want to marry me," he answered lazily. "Or, maybe I didn't want to marry her. What difference does it make now? The fact remains that for whatever reasons, I married you."

"I had always wondered why you picked me when you could have had anyone. But now I think I understand. You married me because no one else would have been stupid enough to put up with you—with your crazy distrust of women, and your philandering. I thought women would be breaking down your door—you're so damned handsome. And they were, but you never gave any of them enough time to see your paranoid personality, did you? So when you *had* to marry, you picked someone who wasn't a looker, someone other men might not want. Someone who'd be grateful because you saved her from a life of spinsterhood. Grateful enough to accept being two-timed. Well, I'm sorry, Congressman, I don't feel very grateful right now. Did you think you could have your wife and lover both?''

Brad pushed her toward the bed causing her to fall backward across it. He dropped on top of her, pinning her body beneath his. "Let's get a couple of things straight. First, this marriage to you was not my idea. So I didn't pick you out as you say." Gail started to reply but Brad covered her mouth with his hand. "Second, I've never indicated in any way I thought you were unattractive. You've always been a pretty woman. You just never bothered to look in the mirror and take stock of your natural assets. Until recently, that is. But to be honest, I think maybe I liked you better when you weren't quite so beautiful."

He took his hand from her mouth. "And third, do you honestly think I'd risk a Senate seat by carrying on with Judith? Or any other woman for that matter. That hardly makes sense, does it?''

Gail was befuddled. Brad was right—if he would go to the extreme of marrying to get elected, he certainly wouldn't foul things up by running around on his wife. "But what was that kiss all about then?" Gail hadn't realized she'd spoken aloud.

"I would have been happy to tell you if you'd just asked me like a mature adult. But frankly, right now, I don't think you deserve an explanation." He sat upright on the side of the bed and ran his fingers through his hair. "I'm sick of your insecurities, your accusations."

"You're a fine one to talk! Always questioning my whereabouts. Always suspecting me of carrying on with Dave. Is that your idea of mature?"

"Maybe not. But I don't want to talk about Dave right now. Let's get back to the subject at hand."

"The subject at hand was your hands all over Judith DeWitt. Just what's your explanation for that—and this time, leave out all those lies you were feeding me a few minutes ago," Gail said bitingly.

"God, what are you going to accuse me of next? Considering the amount of money you've spent on shoes and clothes, it sure can't be trying to keep you barefoot and pregnant."

"Oh no, not barefoot. And certainly not pregnant either. Since I happen to be smart enough to know what it takes to get pregnant. One small display of affection in a marriage won't produce many heirs!"

"You're the one who wanted the platonic arrangement. And I think you're the one who's begging for the agreement to be rescinded. Very well, Gail, I accede," and his lips crushed her ferociously. Her robe had parted and she could feel his bare flesh against her chest.

Gail was amazed at how closely anger and passion were intertwined, for the moment Brad's lips touched hers, she knew he had been right. She wanted him, wanted him desperately. There was a hunger within her that had gone unsated all her adult years until that brief encounter in New Orleans, which had only whetted her appetite. She could no longer postpone her destiny. Nothing mattered any longer, not Judith, not the campaign, not tomorrow. Nothing mattered but Brad's sensuous exploration of her. His touch became gentle, tender, their heated bodies moving together as all reality became submerged in an explosion of love.

CHAPTER EIGHT

"GET UP, WOMAN!" Gail felt a pillow hit her back and she opened her eyes to find Brad standing over her. What time was it anyway she wondered? Brad looked as though he'd been up for hours. He was dressed in gray jogging shorts and a matching sweatshirt. She pulled the bedcovers over her head and groaned.

Brad yanked the covers back and took her hand, pulling her toward him and giving her a good-morning kiss. "We gotta get moving. It's after twelve and we're going to Baton Rouge today, remember? You've got work to do."

Gail reluctantly headed toward the bathroom. Brad was right. Today was an important day—the long-awaited fund-raiser being hosted by Giles LeBeaux to benefit the campaign. The gala held promise of needed capital for last-ditch radio and television advertising. Because Merton Ramsey seemed to have bottomless coffers, the money was crucial. Even though Brad was gaining in the polls, a media blitz by Ramsey could overcome all their efforts. Brad had to be able to match him on radio and television—campaign spot for campaign spot.

Gail ate a late breakfast, spent a couple of hours working, then started getting dressed. She wanted to devote a lot of attention to her appearance today. She knew there would be plenty of press around as well as plenty of Louisiana money and she had to look her best. By five she was ready—wearing a gray-blue draped sheath creation with silver threads running through the fabric. Brad had given her another gift of jewelry, a narrow circlet of diamonds, which she wore around her neck.

She smiled as Brad walked into the bedroom. He reached for his tuxedo jacket in the closet. Gail looked back in the mirror and sighed proudly. Did it really matter what she wore? Who would be able to take their eyes off her handsome husband?

Sometimes Gail felt that living in Louisiana was like being caught in a time warp, as though she were living in two centuries at once. Tonight, especially. Giles had chosen the restored riverboat, the *Mississippi Queen*, as the site of the party. The guests were to board at Baton Rouge and cruise down the Mississippi to New Orleans. Carriages would pick the group up near the Jackson Square levee and take them to the Monteleone Hotel where they would spend the night. The next morning, a chartered party bus would transport everyone back to Baton Rouge, though Gail and Brad would just spend the night at the town house.

The brilliant white paddleboat made Gail think of the musical *Showboat*. Twinkling lights outlined three passenger tiers and the square wheelhouse on top. As she and Brad drove up River Road toward the dock, she could hear the sound of the calliope, beckoning all to come aboard.

As she and Brad boarded, Giles gave them a welcoming hug, wrapping them together in one of his massive bear hugs. Giles was dressed in a white suit with a small American flag in his lapel. He gestured them toward deck chairs where guests sat and sipped mint juleps. Gail looked at the few women already on board. Several, including Giles's wife, Angelina, were dressed in hoop-skirted period dresses.

Angelina didn't join them in the receiving line. She performed her hostess duties more casually, mingling and chatting informally. Gail envied Angelina's not having to stand in line. Even though it was twilight, the heat was stifling, and Gail wished she could sneak away and join the celebration. But she knew she couldn't. Instead, she had to remain by Brad's side, smile pasted on her face.

Gail had perfected a political smile. That toothy, bubbly, smile that didn't quite reach the eyes. She didn't like this part of politics. This was too public for the privacy-loving Gail. But Brad seemed to be in his element. He laughed, joked, and greeted each guest intimately with some small detail about family or business. Often he would bring up some joint experience from years earlier.

Gail was impressed with her husband's memory—his attention to and grasp of detail. How many people could remember having lunch at an out-of-the-way café, or getting stuck in a remote fishing cabin ten years before? Yet Brad recounted dozens of such memories as he shook hands with several hundred guests who had paid a thousand dollars each to attend his fete.

Judith DeWitt was one of the last to come aboard before the anchor was pulled. She kissed both Giles and Brad, and turning to Gail, put her arms around her. Gail froze. It was impossible for her to be warm and hospitable to Judith, but the other woman didn't seem to mind, or even to notice, for that matter. She was effervescent. By her side was a tall, dark man, with hair even blacker than Judith's and eyes like midnight. He took Gail's hand in his and kissed it gallantly.

"Has Brad told you our good news?" Judith bubbled. She held her hand up to Gail and revealed a mammoth diamond engagement ring. "Rene has finally given in." She took the man's arm and squeezed her body to his.

"We're being married as fast as I can arrange it." There was no mistaking Judith's happiness and when she turned to Gail again, the smile she gave her was one of genuine affection.

After the couple strolled on, Brad explained quietly. "Judith stopped by last night to tell me Rene had finally proposed. Ever since we shared a sandbox as children, I've heard nothing but Rene, Rene, Rene from that woman," he smiled. "They must have fallen in love when they were in diapers." He shook his head when Gail shot him a sympathetic look. "Gail, I've never been in love with Judith. I love her, yes—like a sister. But that's all. Can't you accept that?"

Gail nodded. She had no reason to doubt what he was saying. But she wanted to hear more about Judith and Rene. A few more guests came aboard and Gail and Brad greeted them politely. "Why did it take so long for them to finally get together?" Gail asked when they had a free moment. Most guests had arrived, and it seemed the last few were trickling aboard.

"They had been planning to wed, but had a silly misunderstanding and Judith married Linus DeWitt, a Northerner, impulsively on the rebound," Brad explained. "Even though the marriage lasted only a couple of years, Rene wouldn't forgive. It took years for them to reconcile. The problem standing between them was Rene's pride—and Judith's money." Gail was intrigued.

"She could do little about his pride—what had happened had happened. She couldn't undo the fact she'd married a Yankee. But she could take care of the big settlement she'd received from Linus DeWitt, which Rene resented—and she set about contributing it to worthy causes. One of them happened to be my campaign. Finally when Rene saw she was willing to risk her security for love of him, he gave in.'' Gail suddenly felt foolish for feeling such jealousy over Judith all this time. It had been a sisterly kiss she'd witnessed the night before. Judith had wanted only to share her happiness with those she cared about:

When the last guests had boarded, Giles directed the captain to pull anchor. Gail slipped away from the men and sat alone in a deck chair to rest her feet and watch the Louisiana scenery slip by. They steamed slowly past the Old Pentagon Barracks with its double galleries and Doric columns. Gail leaned forward for a better look. She was fascinated with the old structure, having read that it dated back to 1822 and had served as both army barracks and dormitories for Louisiana State University. The famous World War II "Flying Tiger," General Clair Chennault had lived in the barracks while a student at Louisiana State and a statue of the native Louisianan graced the grounds.

Her history lesson was interrupted by the figure of Judith hovering over her. "Mind if I join you?"

Gail was shocked. Judith was the last person she expected to see. She gestured toward the chair beside her. "Where's Rene?"

Judith laughed. "Right now he's in the clutches of Giles LeBeaux. Literally and figuratively. I think they're working up a fishing expedition."

Gail laughed too. She knew how Giles could envelop a person, to the exclusion of everyone else.

Judith sat down next to Gail. Her voice was now serious. "Don't you think it's high time we buried the hatchet and became friends?"

"I wasn't aware we were enemies," Gail lied, trying to cover her discomfort in the face of Judith's confrontation.

"You weren't?"

"Well, maybe we weren't friends or anything like that, but we weren't fighting."

"And you didn't resent me, just a teeny bit?"

"Well," Gail frowned, "maybe a little." She frowned again. "Maybe a lot."

"Gail," Judith sat upright in her chair, legs sidesaddle toward Gail. "I have to be honest with you. I knew how you felt and I just let you keep feeling that way."

Gail started to interrupt, but Judith stopped her. "You see, even though Brad and I have always been just friends, I was jealous of you, afraid you would take my good friend, my confidant away from me. So I let you think the wrong thing about me. In fact, I even encouraged those feelings. Led you on. Will you let me say I'm sorry?"

"I'm really the one who should be apologizing," Gail admitted. "I never gave you a chance."

"Maybe we both were wrong," Judith said.

"Yes, I guess we both were." Gail smiled. "And you know what?—you were never in danger of losing Brad's friendship. Or anything of Brad. He and I are not your average young marrieds."

Judith laughed. "Oh, I know about your marriage." When Gail registered surprise, she quickly added, "Don't worry, Brad didn't tell me, not directly, that is. I just figured it out. The answers he *didn't* give me were answer enough. My hardheaded friend just didn't realize he would fall in love with you, that he would become trapped by his own feelings."

Gail scoffed. "You don't know your friend as well as you think. He doesn't love me. His feelings for me range from indifference to contempt, depending on his mood."

"Don't be too sure, Gail. I know what I'm talking about. In fact...." Just then Brad appeared, obviously surprised to see the two women deep in conversation.

"Well, the two loveliest women on board alone together. What a waste."

"Ever the diplomat, Brad," Judith twitted. "But I guess I'd better find my darling Rene before he gets too far away. I don't intend to lose him again." She rose from her chair and motioned Brad to take her place. "See you later." Judith winked at Gail.

Brad slid into the deck chair beside Gail and handed her a drink—a tall, cool glass of club soda adorned with a lemon slice and a sprig of mint. At the moment, Gail could have used something stronger. Her talk with Judith had left her unsettled and confused. Could Judith have been right about Brad's feelings? What was she going to say before Brad interrupted? Gail took a sip of the club soda as she dwelled on the woman's words.

Brad interrupted her thoughts. "Did you girls have a nice talk?" he quizzed.

Gail looked into her glass. "As a matter of fact we did. Oh, there's the capitol," she said with forced enthusiasm, changing the subject. In the distance, Gail could see the state capitol, rising like a beacon, thirty-four floors above the city. It was America's tallest state capitol building, an impressive sight from the boat.

"Anything I should know about?"

"Oh, nothing really. I just told her what I really thought of her, and that we didn't need her campaign money."

Brad's face paled dramatically as he gasped, "You didn't!"

"No, I didn't," Gail laughed. "But that ought to teach you to be so nosy."

"I owe you one," Brad threatened, and they both laughed.

Brad got up from his chair and offered Gail a hand. "We need to mingle, though I'd much rather sit here with you."

"Why, thank you." Her voice showed surprise. Was he offering her another compliment?

The upbeat Dixieland music of the riverboat's band drifted out behind them over the churning water as the boat headed toward New Orleans. Gail leaned on the railing, entranced as she observed the beautiful antebellum mansions along the river-front. The large graceful homes, enhanced by manicured lawns and huge magnolia trees, faced the water like proud reminders of days gone by.

In the bayous feeding the river, she could see the eerie cypress trees, strung with fringes of Spanish moss. As the river carried them downstream past Lutcher-La Place and Vacherie, Gail was witness to both wealth and poverty. This was typical of Louisiana—a state of contrasts, a haunting, romantic, mysterious state—much like the man she had married. She realized why she had agreed to the marriage of convenience. She truly believed that Brad's contributions in the Senate could lead to a better life for these people—rich and poor alike, to help them preserve the beauty of their land and lead them into the future. And in some small way, perhaps she would be partially responsible. It was a worthy task.

Gail realized that she and Brad had been standing there for a long time, each lost in thought. She smiled at him. "Brad, why don't you go on in without me. I just need another moment, please. Then I'll join you."

GILES HAD ARRANGED the cruise as a combination social and political gathering and had provided a variety of entertainment. There was a jazz combo from the French Quarter of New Orleans and a country and western band from Shreveport. Dancers from the Delta Ballet and actors from a small theater group in Baton Rouge performed in the show room. Artists were on hand to draw caricatures, and some displayed crafts to the guests.

Every half hour or so, Brad would make a brief speech, moving from one area of the boat to another, sending his message to all the guests. The message was always the same: environmental protection and saving Louisiana from Merton Ramsey. The guests were polite and quietly responsive to Brad's positions. There was none of the cheering or loud clapping that usually symbolized Brad's rallies or partisan gatherings, but still the reaction was gratifying. Gail knew checks would follow in a day or so from those who were heeding her husband's urgings for better representation.

It was past two in the morning when the last guests departed the paddleboat in New Orleans. The giant vessel now stood empty and dark as it swayed gently in the summer night.

Gail, Brad, Giles and Angelina stood on the dock. "Thanks, old friend," Brad said to Giles, clasping his arm as he gave him a warm handshake.

"My pleasure, Brad," Giles answered politely. His voice grew harsh, "I have as much interest as you in defeating Merton Ramsey. It makes my blood boil to think of that unprincipled incompetent in the Senate. Why, I'd like to have five minutes alone with that slippery, contemptible, corrupt—"

"Okay, okay," Brad laughed, "I wish you could have those five minutes, too. I think the only thing left of my worthy opponent would be that fuzz on his lip he calls a mustache. But it's been too nice an evening to spoil talking about Merton Ramsey."

"He's right, Giles," Gail added. "We'll worry about Merton tomorrow." She kissed him on the cheek, then Angelina. "Thank you both for a wonderful boat trip."

Gail and Brad walked across the dock then hailed a cab to the town house.

"You were super tonight, Gail," Brad said as they entered the town house. "I think those people would just as soon vote for Mrs. Harrison as her husband what's-his-name," he teased.

"Not a chance. I saw how all the women ogled you. Some of them looked as though they would relish pushing me overboard."

"Jealous?" He took her chin in his fingers and shook it gently.

"Mmmm. Should I be?" Gail slipped out of her shoes. Barefoot she barely reached the middle of his chest. When he pulled her toward him, she took advantage of her position to press her lips against his chest.

"Hey, woman." Brad picked her up and turned toward the stairway.

Gail began giggling. "Dar-r-r-ling—I thought this was only done in the movies." She giggled again, kicking her legs in jest.

"What's so funny about my making love to you? I'm going to wipe that laugh away right now." And with that, Brad's lips came down on hers, not pulling away until the two of them fell upon the bed.

They spent the next month traversing the state as they pursued their joint dream. Even though they were together constantly, they had little time for each other, for intimacy or privacy. The few precious hours alone were for resting from the exhausting pace rather than moments for talking and loving.

But neither Gail nor Brad minded. Despite their new-found feelings for each other, and the harmony that existed between them now, they both knew where their priorities lay—with the campaign and the subsequent demands it placed upon them and their time.

They went north to Monroe and toured the Louisiana Purchase Gardens and Zoo, shaking hands and greeting people, listening to their ideas. The couple occasionally meandered off their assigned route to some secluded town where they would share cornbread and catfish with townspeople and visit farm houses and fishing cabins.

On Sunday mornings, they attended church services with local congregations. Unlike southern Louisiana which was predominantly Catholic, the northern area was mostly protestant, with many Baptists and some Methodists, Presbyterians and Episcopalians.

By the end of the two weeks, they had covered most of the state. Brad had appeared at a peach festival in Ruston, at the Corney Creek Festival in Bernice, toured a new plant near Many and viewed the Civil War battlefield outside of Mansfield.

Gail noticed a weariness about Brad she hadn't seen before. He was usually so energetic, but the hectic campaign schedule seemed to have taken its toll. And no wonder. The routine was enough to wear out a beast of burden, much less a human being. She again asked herself if it was worth it. But she already knew the answer. It took hard work to be elected in a democracy, and good men and women had to take the risks and pay the price. Brad could rest in November if need be, and their marriage, if indeed there was to be a marriage, could be realized then. But not before.

Brad slumped down in the back seat of the limousine and closed his eyes as they drove from the Chamber of Commerce luncheon toward the college. But the respite could only be brief. It was already two forty-five and he was due to speak at the college at three o'clock. The small laugh lines around his eyes were more pronounced. To Gail they looked more like worry lines. She felt guilty, as if she hadn't done her share. But she didn't know what else she could do to help.

Brad reached over and took her hand. "Listen, we'll be finished here around noon tomorrow. Would you mind terribly if I took an early flight back to Washington? Maybe I can get in a little extra sleep before that committee meeting on Monday."

Gail smiled sympathetically. "Of course I don't mind. I'll just hop a flight back to New Orleans. After all, you were only due to be in Louisiana a few hours longer anyway."

"That's true," Brad agreed, "but I had been hoping for a few hours just for us. And now I'm too tired for anything but collapsing."

Gail felt like wrapping him in her arms, but—damn the campaigning—she knew she would muss his hair and her dress if she did so. So she could only squeeze his hand and nod.

He smiled at her through half-closed lids. "You know what I'd like to do when this election is over?"

"Run for President?"

"Very cute, Gail." He laughed. "Woman—don't you even think such thoughts. At least not for a few years, anyway. No, what I'd like to do is to escape to Toledo Bend Lake, fish, read, grow a beard—not think about anything, not even look at a newspaper."

"Sounds awful. You'll probably have withdrawal symptoms." And it doesn't sound like I'm included, Gail thought. But then, why should she be? After all, their agreement only goes up to the election.

"WELCOME BACK, Gail." Aunt Sussy hugged Gail close as the two met at the airport.

"It's good to be home," Gail answered. Home? Did she really say home? A feeling of vulnerability washed over her. She was becoming too attached, starting to care too much.

"Calvin will get your luggage, dear. Let's go on to the car. This heat has taken all my energy."

Gail handed her luggage claim tickets to Calvin as she walked with Aunt Sussy toward the car. Aunt Sussy had bullied her way into a VIP parking spot and the car sat waiting, motor running, watched over by a guard. He helped the women into the car.

"Well," Aunt Sussy's intense blue eyes stared at Gail. "Tell me everything. And don't leave out a single detail."

As ordered, Gail told her everything she could remember about the past month. From the airport to the plantation, through dinner, and even two rounds of after-dinner drinks, she talked.

"Not long ago I couldn't have got a sniff of brandy out of you, much less two glasses. Are you trying to get me drunk to pump information out of me?" Gail laughed.

"Maybe," Aunt Sussy answered. "But so far I haven't got the answers I want. Keep talking."

"What?" Gail gasped. "You've got to be kidding. I've covered every detail almost down to the color of my toe-nail polish. What more do you want?"

"Oh, posh, Gail," Aunt Sussy chided. "You've told me all the official stuff—now I want to hear about you and Bradley."

Gail looked down at her hands. She wasn't surprised at the question. Not really. She just wasn't sure what to say. She smiled at Aunt Sussy. "Fine...everything's fine with us."

Now Aunt Sussy's eyes sparkled. "Really? Oh, Gail, that's marvelous—my dream come true. You and Bradley really together."

"That's not what I meant," Gail said. "I meant we are getting along. Not arguing. But 'really together'? No, I wouldn't go that far."

"Oh." Aunt Sussy rose and walked over to Gail. She patted her shoulder. "Don't you worry, I know everything is going to be just fine—and I mean more than a lack of arguments. Believe me. Well, it's been a long day. Good night, dear."

She left Gail alone with her thoughts—thoughts of Brad and of the possibility of a future with him. Could it be? Could she remain Mrs. Brad Harrison? Or was she fantasizing? Grasping at straws? She knew she loved him, but what kind of commitment did she really have from Brad? True, they had established more than a business relationship, but was it destined to be permanent? She swallowed the last sip of brandy from her glass and made her way to her bedroom, confused and tired.

She left the house early the next morning bound for campaign headquarters. Evelyn was already there going over the results of a recent poll. Brad had made a good choice in sending her to the New Orleans office. She was a tireless worker, a great asset to the Harrison team. "Good morning, Evelyn. How's it going?"

Evelyn looked up. "Gail!" she squealed. "Good to see you again." She came around the desk and hugged Gail. "You and the boss really made some headway last week. Have you seen the polls—Brad's only three points behind."

"Only three points?" Gail clasped her hands together. "You know what? I think we're going to make it!"

"I know," Evelyn laughed. "Isn't it great?"

Dave appeared in the doorway of his office. "Can't a man have any peace and quiet around here? And who's this stranger who's finally returned to do a little work?" He came up to Gail and gave her a quick peck on the cheek.

Gail wrapped an arm around his waist. "Brad didn't tell me you were going to be here."

"I think he wanted to keep me in Washington, but I insisted. I was beginning to get the idea he didn't trust me around you pretty ladies."

"Well I'm glad you're here. There's plenty of work to go around." She smiled up at Dave, a pink glow on her cheeks.

Dave held her at arms' length and gave her a quick inspection. "Gail, I hate to say it but I think Brad must be good for you. You look terrific. Too skinny, maybe, but terrific."

"Too skinny? Me?" Gail put her hands up to her face. "I never thought anyone would ever say such a thing to me." Gail knew the hard campaigning and the energy spent during long, long days had left her little time to eat. Still, Dave's comments made her feel strangely happy, satisfied.

"Well," Dave interrupted her thoughts, "what can we do today? Feel like licking envelopes or passing out Harrison stickers?"

Gail walked over to her desk and thumbed through her calendar. "No appearances today. Great, I don't have to be wifely and demure," she smiled. "Let's just talk and decide what comes next."

"Fine," Dave replied. "Come on into my office and I'll brief you on the latest from Washington. Evelyn, bring those surveys in here with you and we can show Gail how well it's going."

The three of them spent an hour analyzing the figures and predicting what the next few weeks would bring. The intercom buzzed, then Dave handed the phone to Gail. "Your better half is on the phone, Gail. Shall I lie and say we're not working on campaign stuff? I could say we're in here making mad passionate love." He handed the phone to Gail.

"Not funny," Gail said, holding her hand over the mouthpiece. "Brad does not have a sense of humor where you're concerned." She removed her hand. "Hello."

"Gail, hello," Brad's voice was serious. "I didn't expect you back in New Orleans so soon. I thought maybe you'd keep Aunt Sussy company for a few days and get a little rest."

"No, I decided I'd better run down and check on the hired help." Dave and Evelyn shot good-natured frowns her way. "And don't worry, I'm only here for an hour or so before I tend to my wifely chores like buying out the department stores."

"Good girl," Brad said. "Listen, Gail, the reason I called is to tell you I may be up here longer than usual. You wouldn't believe the workload. Things really piled up while we were on the road. Quite a backlog. And I've got a lot of committee work too."

"You're not pushing too hard are you? You don't want to be too pooped to charm the ladies during the wind-down."

"Don't concern yourself with that, my worry-wart wife. I will always have a reservoir of charm to fall back on, no matter how tired I may be."

All too true, she thought. Although he was joking, they both knew he had a real knack for establishing rapport with women. Even if it was on a superficial level. "Well, I'd better let you get back to the committee work. Don't worry about having to stay longer in Washington. I know you can't help it. I guess I'll just have to carry on without you."

"Just make sure you don't carry on *too* well." His voice was calm, but Gail knew he was referring to her and Dave.

"Not to worry," she assured him. "I'll be alone and miserable, counting the minutes until you come back."

"Perfect," Brad said. "Now will you let me talk to Dave a minute?"

As she had promised Brad, Gail left the campaign office within the hour and headed for the stores. Shopping for clothes was becoming a routine for her. It was difficult to remember why she had shied away from fashionable clothes in the past. Or what had motivated her to think she had to dress drably in order to be respected for her intelligence.

The new Gail relished the time trying on clothes. Everything looked good on her petite frame. She remembered her high school and college graduations, being thankful the cap and gown disguised her figure. She wondered what her classmates would think of her now. Gail wished a few of the cheerleader types could see her trying to decide between the pink georgette sheath or the jade silk shirtwaist. They wouldn't even recognize her, she decided.

"Take both of them" a voice behind her said. "They both look terrific."

"Judith!" Gail exclaimed. "I didn't see you over there."

"I know," Judith laughed. "I was sitting on the couch waiting for my fitter and just watching you. I'm so fascinated with your transformation from the Gail I met months ago that I had to just stare silently." She smiled. "I didn't mean to be spying on you."

"That's okay," Gail responded. "It's nice to know someone is that interested in how I look." She giggled. "I'm not used to it. I haven't been this way for very long."

"Well, it doesn't matter how long it's been—the important thing is how you are now." Judith looked behind Gail's shoulder. "There's my fitter. Say, how about my buying you lunch this week?"

"Great," Gail answered. "Wednesday okay?"

"Fine. I'll call you then." She kissed Gail on the cheek. "'Bye now."

Gail watched Judith head for the fitting room. She turned to the saleslady, "I'll take both dresses."

It was a hot morning as Gail and Aunt Sussy sat on the bricked patio sipping coffee, reading the morning papers.

"Look at this," Gail said. "The unemployment rate rose two percent this month. That's terrible."

"Yes, dear," Aunt Sussy mumbled, not looking up from her paper. She turned the page. "Oh my."

"Anything wrong?" Gail asked.

"No, Gail, nothing." She turned back to her paper.

Fifteen minutes passed, then Gail asked, "Are you ever going to turn loose of that section?"

Aunt Sussy looked up warily. "I'm not through with it yet. Why don't you go get dressed while I finish."

Gail sighed. "You know I always finish the paper before I do anything. What's so interesting about the national section today?"

Aunt Sussy looked agitated. "There's a lot more to it than usual, I guess. Why don't you look at the sports section?"

Now Gail was feeling agitated. "You know I hate sports. What's come over you this morning?"

"Nothing." She rose from the table. "I think I'll take my paper inside where I can read in peace." She left abruptly before Gail could say anything.

Gail's eyes followed her into the house. Now wasn't that the darnedest thing? Aunt Sussy wasn't acting like herself at all. Maybe the heat was getting to her, Gail decided. She finished her cup of coffee then got up from her chair. She might as well go in and get dressed, she told herself. There was no more newspaper to read anyway.

It was Wednesday and Gail had planned to have lunch with Judith today. The phone rang just as she was heading for her bedroom.

"Hello, Gail, hope I didn't wake you." It was Judith.

"No problem," Gail answered. "Aunt Sussy and I have been up for hours. We just finished reading the paper." Or most of it anyway, she thought.

"You're putting me to shame," Judith admitted. "I haven't even opened my eyes completely yet. But, anyway, I promise to be awake before lunch. How about Brennan's?"

Gail arranged to meet Judith at twelve. She was looking forward to spending some time in the French Quarter since the campaign had robbed her of much chance for sight-seeing in New Orleans. She could spend the entire afternoon browsing through shops and museums. Maybe Aunt Sussy would be out of her strange mood by the time she returned.

Gail strolled down Rampart Street heading toward Brennan's. She was a few minutes early so she took advantage of the extra time to peer into little shops and private courtyards.

A ceramic rabbit in an antique shop caught her eye. It had raised pink rosebuds on its shiny white body and its tail was a larger rosebud. Gail loved rabbits. This one would be a perfect addition to the collection she had back in Washington. Each rabbit was a souvenir of some special time in her life or a special place she visited—this one would remind her of Louisiana.

Gail entered the store to examine the rabbit more closely. "Morning ma'am." An elderly man sat behind the counter reading a newspaper. "Can I help you with something?"

"I just want a closer look at that rabbit." Not bad, Gail decided and carried the rabbit over to the cash register.

"A nice choice," the old storekeeper said, rising from his chair. He laid his paper on the counter. "Excuse me a minute while I find a box for this bunny."

As she waited, Gail looked down at the paper. Even upside down, she could recognize him. Brad. In a photograph. Who was that woman with him? Gail snatched the paper up and righted it. She examined the picture and the caption underneath it which read: Congressman Harrison at reception.

According to the brief article, Brad was putting in a hard day's night with the daughter of an ambassador from South America. Needless to say, the daughter was beautiful and apparently quite fond of Brad the way she was smiling at him.

"Committee work," was it? Poor guy, she thought bitterly. His black-tie affairs never seem to end. The man would just be partied to death by the time he got back to Louisiana.

Tears of fury filled her eyes and Gail wiped them away quickly as the storekeeper returned with a small box. She kept her emotions in check as she paid for the purchase and left the shop. It was exactly twelve o'clock. Judith would be waiting.

The thought of being calm and polite over lunch filled Gail with panic. She wanted to escape, to go somewhere and gather her thoughts. She also wanted desperately to call Brad and tell him exactly what she was feeling at this moment—humiliation and hurt. How dare he lie to her? Tell her he was working night and day and then carry on with some young cutie. Especially where he would be seen. If he didn't think much of his relationship with Gail, at least he could have remembered the campaign. What would Merton Ramsey think of all this? What would that conniver do with this information?

Gail's mind flitted back and forth from the campaign to her marriage and life with Brad, and back to the campaign. She felt stabs of pain no matter what subject she thought about, her sense of betrayal making her head hurt with rage. She had allowed the campaign to take precedence over everything, including her own feelings about Brad, when he apparently didn't give a flip about his reputation. He'd got himself in a quandary early in the campaign and had ended up married to Gail as a result. Was he now going to jeopardize everything with some silly fling? It didn't seem like the Brad she'd come to know—he was so image conscious—but then again she remembered the incident in Georgetown. That didn't sound like the Brad she'd come to know either. Or did she know him? Could she simply be deluding herself there, too? Sure things had changed between them, but Brad had made no promises, had spoken no words about love or the possibility of a real marriage.

Gail arrived at the restaurant just as Judith was walking up from the other direction. Lunch was no longer appealing but Judith was still a vital contributor to the campaign. Also, she was Brad's friend and Gail could not afford to offend her. Especially since the woman had extended an olive branch of friendship to Gail. It would be thoughtless and rude to cancel.

"Perfect timing," Judith exclaimed, giving Gail a hug. "I'm starved. How about you?"

"Maybe after a Bloody Mary, " Gail answered as they were escorted to their seats. Maybe after ten Bloody Marys, she thought miserably. I'll need them to carry on this pretense of the happy wife with Judith.

"Well, how's the campaign going?" Judith was seated across from Gail at a corner table for two.

"So-so," Gail replied noncommittally.

"Well, I think Ramsey's beginning to run scared." Judith picked up a bread stick and started spreading it with butter. "Did you see that silly picture in today's newspaper?"

Gail was taken aback, curious to hear what Judith had to say about it. "Huh, no. Aunt Sussy seemed determined to hoard the front page this morning."

"Maybe she was afraid it would upset you. Aunt Sussy is such a romantic it probably never occurred to her that you'd see through that picture right away."

"Well, tell me about it." Gail was beginning to feel foolish.

"Ramsey's own paper—he's actually Chairman of the Board—ran this picture of Brad with a woman. The jerk did a little plastic surgery on a photograph to try to embarrass Brad. You know, trying to make it look like a little tête-à-tête. Only I'm positive the picture was cut from a group scene. If you looked closely you could even see someone else's hand on her waist. I'm tempted to get a copy of the whole picture and send it to the *Times Picayune*."

"But not everyone's as politically observant as you, Judith." Me, for instance, thought Gail. "Do you think it will hurt Brad's image?"

"Not in the long run. Don't worry about it, Gail. If I know Brad, he can probably use this to his advantage and expose Ramsey for the character assassin he really is. Any bad publicity will likely just backfire on Ramsey."

Aunt Sussy was on the telephone when Gail returned from New Orleans. "Yes, Bradley, she's just come in," Aunt Sussy handed the telephone to Gail. "It's for you, dear."

"Thank you," Gail said and her voice changed to a soft seductive tone as she answered. "Yes?"

"You've been out?" Brad's voice was icy.

"Yes, I had lunch at Brennan's."

"Right. Is there anything new?" Brad sounded annoyed, almost angry.

"Nothing except the latest issue of Ramsey's paper. That hasn't upset you, has it?"

She could hear him sigh over the phone. "It wouldn't have except for your reaction. Gail, it's not what you think. I can explain that picture. It was no reason for you to go running to Dave."

Gail was silent. Dave? What was Brad talking about?

"Did you hear what I said?" he asked. He sounded miserable.

"I heard," she answered. "But I don't know what you're talking about."

"I'm talking about the fact that the two of you have been out of reach all day. It doesn't take a genius to figure out you were together," Brad snarled. "You being seen too often with Dave could do as much damage as that stupid picture."

"What kind of accusation are you making this time, Brad? Because I don't like what you're getting at."

"Dammit, Gail, I don't need this from you. I'm up to my eyebrows in committee work and campaigning and don't relish domestic problems to boot." He paused. "Of course, women generally cause trouble at the most inopportune time, don't they?"

Before he could continue, Gail hung up the receiver. She hurried out of the den and headed for the stairs. The phone began ringing. "Shall I get that?" Aunt Sussy's voice rang out from the sitting room.

"Yes," Gail shouted from the stairs. "But I'm not home—to anyone." She retreated to her room before Aunt Sussy could intercept her. She'd had enough of Brad and his distrust. That she'd earlier spent a few hours agonizing over her own distrust wasn't at issue. After all, she'd quickly understood her error as soon as Judith had pointed it out. But with Brad, there was no convincing him she and Dave were simply good friends. She might as well give up trying.

CHAPTER NINE

THE DAY PASSED BY slowly, the evening even slower. Gail remained in her room, coming out only to take a long slow walk around the gardens. She was trying to clear her head, to decide what she was going to do during the weeks remaining in Brad's campaign. She knew she had to see it through to its conclusion. She had to remain Brad's wife until the votes were in and the winner declared. But she didn't have to live with him or be with him. Not any more than necessary. If the past twenty-four hours had taught her anything, it was that a future with Brad was impossible. She could no longer handle his distrust of her and she was just as bad, ready at the drop of a hat to think the worst of him. What was wrong with the two of them anyway? Neither seemed really willing to give the other a chance.

Gail was curled up on the sofa in her bedroom when she heard the sound of tires on the gravel driveway. She looked out the window. Dave. He was just getting out of his car. What was he doing here? Had Brad said something to him? Gail hoped not. She really didn't think Dave would be forgiving again. It had taken him a while to put the incident about the brooch behind him. He might not stand for any more of Brad's accusations. And Brad needed Dave—he was a valuable friend and a tireless campaigner.

Gail went to the dresser and brushed her hair. A quick application of lip gloss and she looked almost presentable—except for her red-rimmed eyes. She strode out of the bedroom and down the stairs. She might as well go down and find out what this was about.

"Hello, Dave." She greeted him in the hallway. "Would you like to join me in the study?"

Dave nodded and followed her into the room.

"Can I fix you a drink?"

"No, thanks." Dave sat down. "Gail, Brad asked me to come out. He needs you in Washington to do some work for him. He needs help on the legislation. Will you go?"

"Brad asked you to come here?"

Dave nodded.

"Did he say anything else? Anything about—"

"He said a lot, Gail—a lot of nonsense. Something about us being together incommunicado. If the conversation hadn't been by telephone, we'd probably have come to blows. But I set him straight—told him I'd been in meetings all day in Lake Charles. That I hadn't seen you and that he was a damned fool!" Dave leaned forward in his chair. "Will you go to Washington? I think Brad will be pleased if you do."

Gail doubted that. She wasn't sure why Brad wanted her with him, but whatever his motive, maybe it was better accepting the request than staying there, miserable. Anyway, since there were only a few weeks left until the election, she needed to talk to Sam about going back to her job.

"When do we leave?"

Dave rose from the love seat. "Tonight. Pack your bags and I'll drive you to the airport."

Brad was standing at the gate as Gail deplaned at National Airport. The look on his face told her nothing. But she'd decided on the flight up how to handle the next few weeks. She'd be civil—no use adding fuel to the fire—

but she'd keep Brad at arm's length. She'd live up to her obligations as far as the campaign was concerned, but that was it. She and Brad would simply be platonic roommates for the next couple of weeks. "Hello, Brad."

"Hello," he replied grimly, as he relieved her of her flight bag. "We'll talk when we get home."

"I don't think we have anything left to talk about, Brad. I'm here and I'll stick with the campaign through the election. Let's just leave it at that."

Brad looked as though he wanted to protest but he simply led her to a waiting taxi and the two rode in silence to Brad's apartment.

Gail had never been there before. It was a strange sensation, being in a place her husband had called home.

"Your things are in the bedroom," Brad said. "I had them brought over from your apartment."

"Thank you," she answered quietly. She followed him into the room he had indicated. Her eyes fell immediately on her rabbit collection, neatly arranged on a glass étagère. They were all there, twenty-three rabbits—glass, wicker, clay, cloth, even one made out of a piece of driftwood. The only ones missing were the paperweight she kept on her desk and the rosebud rabbit she'd bought yesterday in New Orleans.

"I didn't know you had such a thing for rabbits," Brad admitted as he followed her eyes to the étagère.

"There are a lot of things you don't know about me. But why should you? After all, I'm really only a hired hand, aren't I, on special assignment." The bitterness in her words surprised even Gail.

"Gail, don't start," warned Brad. "Can't we forget that stupid phone call and get back to the business at hand?"

"Business—the one and only reason I'm here—the campaign. I made a commitment to you and to Sam and to myself and I intend to keep it. I intend to see this matter through. You don't need to worry about that."

Brad moved toward her. "Don't come any closer," she warned. "My relationship with you from now on will be strictly *business*. I'll continue to play the dutiful wife in public." She hesitated. "But only in public. As a private couple, we no longer exist. Is that clear?"

"Quite clear," he answered brusquely. "And since it's so late, I'll leave you alone to go to bed. I've still got at least an hour's work to do." Brad slammed the door behind him as he left the room.

Gail sat on the side of the bed, her fury and her bravado now subsiding. She could feel her heart beating against her chest. Even her wrath could not obliterate the love she felt for this man. It would take a long time to rid herself of her feeling for him, if ever, but she would have to try.

"SAM!" Gail ran into his arms. "It's so good to see you again."

Sam had been leaning over a table, studying news clippings when Gail entered Brad's office. He smiled in surprise and in pleasure as Gail greeted him. "Is it really you?" he asked. "My goodness, you look terrific. Stand back and let me take a gander at you."

Gail stood at arm's reach from her former boss and let him look her over. "Well, do I pass muster?"

"And then some," Sam beamed. "I always knew you were pretty, but I guess I didn't realize just how beautiful you actually were."

"Just like a man," Gail laughed. "Always take us women for granted."

"I guess we do at that," he agreed good-naturedly. "We don't appreciate you till you're gone."

"So what are you doing over here today?" she asked. "Still keeping a hand in the action?"

"You know me, Gail. Can't keep this old race horse from the track." He patted her shoulder. "From what my sources and these clippings tell me, you've done a fine job of getting Brad close to a lead position."

"Don't give me so much credit," Gail said quickly. "There are some pretty talented people on Brad's team." She walked over to the coffee maker and poured herself a cup. It was as thick and awful looking as ever. "I'll never get to like this stuff." She grimaced as she took a swallow. And I guess I won't have to, she thought. Not now.

"Give yourself some time," Sam suggested.

"I'm afraid there won't be time for that. The campaign will be over soon and I'll be coming back to Washington, to my old job, remember?" Gail squeezed his arm.

"Is that what you want to do?" Sam looked doubtful.

"Of course. After all, that's the way we planned it."

"Did we?" Sam picked up his pipe from an ashtray on the table.

"Sure we did. I married Brad so he could win an election and when the election is over, then the marriage will be, too."

"Is that the way you want it?" Sam had pulled his tobacco pouch from his jacket pocket and was proceeding to stuff his pipe bowl. His thick eyebrows formed a frown as he went through the motions so familiar to Gail.

"I've done a lot of thinking the past few months—about a lot of things. Sam, I'm twenty-seven years old, almost twenty-eight, and I don't really know myself. But I'm working on it."

"I can see you are, Gail. But why can't you keep working on it with Brad? You two can go a long way together."

"A long way in politics, maybe. But I'm not sure that's what I want to do with the rest of my life. I may go back to school. Perhaps get a teaching degree. I've discovered the political life can be very demanding, and very painful."

"Maybe for some people but surely not for the daughter of Russell Meredith. I didn't take you for a quitter, Gail."

"Oh, Sam, I'm not quitting, I'm growing. Can't you see?"

"All I see is that you're running. Running away from a good thing. And what does Brad think about all this?"

"The same as me. He's probably more anxious to get rid of me than I am to leave."

"Well, let's just see about that. We'll ask him." Ignoring Gail's sputtering protests, Sam pushed her toward Brad's private office. Without bothering to knock, he opened the door and shut it firmly behind him.

"Gail tells me the fuse is burning low on this marriage, that the two of you plan to call it off after the election. Is that right?"

Brad looked up from the papers on his desk. If he were caught off guard, he didn't show it. "I'm seldom privy to the thoughts running through Gail's mind," he said evenly.

"Is this what you want, Brad, what you really want?" Sam's look was stern.

"I want whatever Gail wants," Brad replied.

"And if I ask her, she's going to say 'I want whatever Brad wants.' You are the two most exasperating individuals I've ever met." Sam puffed vigorously on his pipe but it had gone out. He pulled it from his mouth and scowled at it the same way he'd been scowling at them. "All right," he said, "this is it. My patience has run out. Now I'm going to tell you what you both want but are too darned stubborn to admit. Gail, I've known you since you were in diapers and I figured out a long time ago what's going on in your head. I usually know what you're thinking before you do. And I know you love Brad, so why don't you admit it to him? Could make a hell of a lot of difference." He turned to Brad.

"And you, Brad. If you only had the guts to admit the truth. Is it so hard, so difficult, to tell this girl what you're really feeling? Would a simple 'I love you' be so difficult?"

Brad didn't respond. His face was devoid of emotion, a poker face.

"Sam, you've got it all wrong," Gail protested. "Why don't you just give up? You manipulated us once. Twice. But not anymore. We're on to you now." She hurried out of the room into a small back office before Sam could stop her.

It was half an hour later when Sam finally emerged from Brad's office, red-faced and mad, mumbling something about "the darned younger generation." He muttered a grumpy goodbye to Gail as he rushed out the doors.

Gail remained working the rest of the afternoon and into the early evening, sorting through proposals and comments from constituents and staff. She'd managed to produce six pages for Brad's position paper despite the emotional upheaval she felt. Gail hadn't seen Brad since Sam left. What on earth had he thought about Sam's pronouncements? What did she think? Did Brad really love her? She wished it were true, but she couldn't imagine what had given Sam such an idea. Maybe an old man's delusions. Well, she'd tried to tell him he was mistaken. He could have saved a lot of time by listening to her.

At six-thirty the door to Brad's office opened and he came out, tie loosened at the neck and coat held casually over one shoulder. "Ready to go home, darling?" he said. No sarcasm was evident in his tone, even to Gail.

Gail began to tidy the desk, at the same time stuffing papers into a briefcase. "Just give me a couple of seconds," she answered sweetly. She could be just as phony as her husband, especially in front of the two secretaries still laboring in the outer office. They exchanged endearing looks, amorous words as Brad took her arm and they walked out together.

But once they stepped into the hall, his voice deepened. "Would it be asking too much for you to make an appearance with me tonight at a State Department reception?"

"I told you," she answered, "that I'd fulfill all my campaign obligations. I'd be delighted to go that reception with you."

"Do you think you might be able to go so far as pretending you're enjoying yourself?"

Brad was smiling when they entered the crowded reception together. It was a sophisticated affair; there was a mish-mash of State Department officials, politicians and foreign dignitaries in attendance. Brad and Gail mingled with them all, glasses of champagne helping to keep conversation flowing.

Gail looked lovely, her appearance a contradiction to her inner feelings. With Aunt Sussy's help, she had acquired an entire wardrobe of appropriate reception garb and tonight she was dressed in a strapless silk cranberry-colored dress and matching jacket. Gail was wearing the gem necklace Brad had given her in spite of her misgivings. But the necklace was pretty and its sparkle did enhance the simple lines of the outfit.

The Harrisons made a dazzling couple, both blond, both lightly tanned. Gail thought wryly how smashing they would look in divorce court. The idea took her breath away as a wave of depression washed over her.

The minutes seemed to pass interminably as they performed their social and professional obligations, but finally Brad signaled to Gail with a slight nod of his head that they could leave.

The skies had opened over Washington and a downpour drummed against the car as they headed toward the apartment. The swish of the windshield wipers was the only sound in the car as they rode silently in the night. Brad parked in front of the apartment building, and they sat staring at the steady rain making rivulets down the windows.

The tension was becoming unbearable as the two waited impatiently for the rain to let up. But it seemed as if there were to be no end to this shower.

Brad looked at Gail. "Well, what do you think? Are we destined to be here all night?"

"I'm ready to make a run for it," Gail answered, reaching for the door handle. She jumped from the car and raced up the sidewalk to the front door. Brad was only steps behind her and reached around her to unlock the door. The short run had soaked them both.

They stepped into the hall, water running down their faces and dripping onto the terrazzo tile. "Ladies first," Brad gestured to the upstairs bathroom. "I'll change down here."

Gail took off her shoes as she climbed up the carpeted stairway to the bathroom. Her silk dress hung limply against her body, and large dark circles were forming where the water had penetrated the material. Her blond hair also hung in wet spikes and her waterproof mascara had failed the test. Black streaks had formed under each eye.

Gail turned on the bathroom light and glanced into the mirror. "I'm a mess," she said aloud as her earlier good feelings about her appearance vanished with the soaking. She stood staring at her reflection, frozen into inactivity as Brad came up behind her, his velour robe having already replaced his wet evening clothes.

"What's the matter?" he asked.

Gail turned around in surprise. She had been lost in a daze, not realizing how long she had been standing mesmerized. "Nothing," she answered meekly. Her face bore an expression of total forlornness, so sad that Brad began laughing.

"You look terrible," he said. "Just like a little lost waif."

"Thanks," she grumbled good-naturedly. "For once, we agree on something. I look like something the cat dragged in." She reached for a tissue to wipe her face.

"Let me do that," he offered, and began wiping the makeup from under her eyes. Gail stood quietly, not really knowing how to act in the face of the unexpected gesture.

"There. That's better." Brad handed her the tissue. "But you had better get out of those clothes." He placed a hand on her wet shoulder. Then suddenly, without warning, he leaned down and planted a gentle kiss on her lips.

Gail looked up at him, shock and wonder on her face as he kissed her a second time and pulled her up into his arms. "But I'm all wet," she protested.

Brad smiled, "What's a little water between friends?" He led her into the bedroom. "Now let's get rid of that damp dress." Before she could utter a word, his fingers began to undo the zipper.

The clothes came off quickly and effortlessly and Brad removed his robe in two quick motions. He was nude and his body felt warm against her own, still cold and damp from the rain.

Their lovemaking was intense and desperate, a desperation born out of frustration and denial. For weeks, Gail and Brad had been ignoring pent-up passions, and those passions, once unleashed knew no boundaries.

He was a sensitive lover, so tender and caring. Gail had never known the kind of pleasure Brad was able to instill in her.

Afterward they lay together still and silent, until they both fell into a deep sleep.

When Gail awoke, she was alone in bed. She pulled on a robe and headed downstairs in search of Brad. But he wasn't there. That's strange, she thought.

She made a pot of coffee and sat down to scan the newspapers stacked on the breakfast bar, but she couldn't concentrate. She and Brad had just shared a special night together; she felt closer to him then ever, and for the first time in weeks she dared to feel optimistic. Maybe Sam was right.

But as she continued to sip her coffee and reflect on the night before, she came to the conclusion that nothing had changed. She and Brad had exchanged feelings of passion—but did that really mean anything? Their sex was probably nothing more than a release of tension for Brad; he couldn't have other women while married to Gail. She was a convenience—very appropriate for this kind of marriage.

Gail realized there had been no declaration of love, no resolution of the conflict that cut to the core of their relationship. What it boiled down to was a lack of commitment. Of course they could never work things out. Why had she thought they could?

The phone rang. It was Brad. "I didn't have the heart to wake you. I'm at the office."

"It figures," she said, her voice flat.

"You don't sound very chipper. Are you mad? Have I done something?" Brad asked.

"No, I'm not mad. And no, you haven't done anything," she answered. That was the problem, she told herself.

"Well, this obviously isn't a good time for you. We'll talk later." He was irritated. Gail knew it. She also knew she had managed to convey the frustration she felt, the frustration which now hung heavy.

For the next week, Gail and Brad operated as a team, sharing the same apartment and working together at the congressional office, and spending their nights locked in each others' arms. They were together constantly, united in their purpose, but something was missing. The only conversation between them involved the campaign. During the gatherings they attended, they smiled and cooed at each other and no one was the wiser that the newlyweds weren't a deliriously happy couple. But behind the false front, Gail was miserable, and she couldn't help feeling Brad was also. Only at night, when they were together in bed, did she feel safe and secure. She might not have Brad's love, but being in his arms sure eased the pain and emptiness she was feeling.

The only one sensitive to their misery was Sam. But he had made himself scarce since the discussion in Brad's office. Gail guessed what was troubling him. He could see through their public demeanor and was disappointed his devious little scheme hadn't worked, and now he was a frustrated Cupid who'd failed to bring Gail and Brad together on a permanent basis. He was upset because the couple hadn't worked matters out better than they had. Sam wasn't used to failure.

GAIL SAT at her desk drinking a cola and leafing through Brad's official photograph album. She needed a short break. Brad was still in his office, though the rest of the staff had left for the day. The pictures covered every aspect of his career—a visual chronicle of his days as a congressman. There was one of Brad receiving a pen from the president after a bill was signed, and one of Brad kissing a baby in Alexandria, another of him being sworn into the House, and a nice shot of Brad and Sam standing on the capitol steps.

Stuck in the back was a folder of new pictures not yet arranged. Gail pulled them out and began flipping through them. She was astonished. Most of the pictures were of her—one with Brad at Giles's first party and then on the riverboat, one of her and Brad campaigning at the rose gardens in Shreveport, another of the two of them strolling through the French Quarter in New Orleans and several of Gail alone. Brad walked up behind her.

"Enjoying your publicity photos?"

"I guess I am. What are all these Brad?"

"Just a few pictures I wanted to save. Do you have any objections?"

"No, but they won't have much purpose in a few weeks."

"Is that how you see it, Gail?"

"It's what we knew all along, isn't it?"

"Yes, I guess so," Brad said. Was Gail imagining it or was there a hesitation in his voice?

"So where do we go from here?"

Brad shook his head. "I'm not sure. All I know is we have a good working relationship and the time is not right for these kinds of discussions. Can't we just table them for a while?''

"Certainly," Gail answered. She knew what he meant. Keep things on hold until the campaign was over. She flipped the cover of the folder shut and shoved it back into the album. "If you'll excuse me, I really do need to get back to the project at hand—my break is over."

Brad shrugged his shoulders and returned to his office.

THE CAMERAS AND PRESS were waiting when Gail and Brad arrived at the New Orleans airport. The campaign countdown had begun—seventy-two hours until the polls opened. Brad would spend these final days with his constituents, reminding them of what he stood for.

Evelyn had astutely arranged this airport gathering. A high school band greeted them with a march. Giles Le-Beaux stood at the gate with a bouquet of flowers for Gail and a hearty handshake for Brad. Ten spirited young girls decked out in red-white-and-blue outfits cheered and clapped as the couple made their appearance in the gate area.

A microphone was thrust into Brad's face. "Well, Congressman, how does it look?" Brad smiled at the interviewer and into the camera and then gave a thumbs-up sign.

"Looking good," he shouted over the din. He pulled Gail closer. "Gail and I think we're going to make it without a runoff." He smiled at Gail and she smiled back at him.

"Of course he's going to make it," Giles echoed, sticking his face into the shot. "Bradley is a shoo-in."

Brad smiled self-consciously. "Well," he corrected, "maybe not a shoo-in, but we feel very good about our chances."

"And you, Mrs. Harrison," the reporter asked Gail.

"Just as my husband says," Gail answered. "Looking good."

After a few more questions the couple walked on and moved through the airport, shaking hands and smiling at potential voters, until they got to the airport doors where Giles's Lincoln Continental and driver awaited them.

The car pulled up in front of the town house where the Harrisons would be staying until the election. Giles and his driver helped them unload. "Well, my old friend," Brad said to Giles, "no matter which way this election goes, I want you to know I'll never forget what you've tried to do for me."

Giles smiled. "What are friends for? Besides I'm no gambler. I know my investment is going to pay off soon. I feel very confident that Ramsey will be forever relegated to the dirt where he belongs." Giles gave Gail a grin and wink. "You and your lovely wife have sealed his fate."

"I'm afraid I can't take the credit," Gail said, embarrassed at Giles's assessment and afraid that Brad would take offense at this attention given her. But he surprised her when he agreed, saying, "You're right, Giles, I couldn't have done it without her." He touched Gail's elbow. "Time to go in, darling."

Gail and Brad entered the foyer silently, the simulated cheerfulness now gone from their faces. *Well, this is the beginning of the end,* she thought. *A few more days and all the pretense will stop. The election will be decided, Brad will be making plans for the next few months and I—I'll be trying to figure out how to get my life back together.* She sighed, suddenly very tired. "I'm going to lie down," she said to Brad. "Call me when it's time to dress for the rally." Gail headed toward the bedroom as Brad mumbled an okay.

The campaign finale was a big blur. Only a few scant minutes were available for soaking aching feet, taking aspirin, and if one were lucky, a few seconds of peace and quiet.

In a way, Gail was grateful for the pandemonium. It meant no arguments, no recriminations and no time alone with Brad. It also meant no time alone with herself to feel remorse or self-pity. Soon it would be over.

Finally it happened. The polls had closed. A small group of loyalists had gathered in the Harrisons' den to watch the returns on television. The phone was ringing constantly with results from poll watchers around the state. Electricity crackled throughout the room each time the television announced even a fraction of a change. The countdown had begun. Downtown a second gathering was beginning to accumulate at the Fairmont. Brad was due there later, either to claim victory or to acknowledge defeat.

Gail sat in a corner chair nervously watching the returns. It was slow going. Ramsey ahead by a thousand votes, then Brad in the lead, then Ramsey and then it became a two-man race, as the other candidates fell far behind. At eight-thirty, Brad took the top position and held it as a ground-swell of votes began flowing in. By ten o'clock it was all over. The television stations declared Brad the winner by a majority and the room erupted into a chaos of back slapping, handshaking, hugging and a round of drinks.

For a long time Gail watched the jubilant crowd with a smile of satisfaction. They'd done it. She'd done it. Her job was complete. As more people began to filter in, she silently stole away from the room and quietly crept up the staircase. She had to leave now. Tonight. Her heart was breaking and she knew if she didn't go immediately, she'd stay until Brad kicked her out. And she couldn't bear that.

She pulled a small bag from the top of the closet—it would do; she'd take only a few things. She was just too weary to do more. Aunt Sussy could send the rest later. Gail twisted her wedding rings from her finger, then lay them on the dressing table where Brad could find them. She wanted no memories of him, no memories other than those that would cling forever to her heart. Languidly, she reached into the top drawer of the bureau.

The bedroom door opened quietly. "Gail, are you about—what's going on?" Brad was frowning, a puzzled look on his face.

"Just living up to my side of the bargain. As you've so often reminded me to do. This marriage had an election-day detonation clause, remember? Congratulations on your victory, Senator. I know nothing's more important to you than winning the election." Her voice was stilted. She could feel tears coming on—her valiant attempt to control her emotions unsuccessful.

"It's *our* victory, Gail," he corrected, "and it would be hollow without you." He took her hand in his. "I don't want you to go."

"Brad, our working relationship is over and I don't want to go on with this loveless marriage...."

"I see." He dropped her hand. "You mean you're going to leave. Just like that."

"Just like that," she echoed.

Brad stared at her, as though unable to comprehend what she was telling him. "Then you don't have any feelings for me at all?"

Gail was surprised at the pain in his voice. He didn't look like a man who'd finally achieved his dream. In fact, he looked just the opposite, hurt and defeated. His vulnerability touched deep into her soul. "Oh, Brad, I *do* love you. I suppose I always have. I love you so much I'm not about to keep you trapped in a marriage you don't want, to a woman you don't love." She turned to the bureau and continued pulling clothes out.

He was by her side in three broad strides, turning her to face him. "But I love you, too, Gail. I've loved you for a long time. And I'm not about to change my mind. Not now, not ever."

"You're just trying to console me. You never—" She was hushed when Brad put his fingers to her lips.

"I was afraid to tell you," he said. "Afraid you didn't feel the same way. But Sam knew...and Aunt Sussy."

Brad picked up the rings lying forsaken on the dressing table and handed them to her. "Please put these back on and never take them off again."

"You mean—you mean you loved me when we married?"

"Well, maybe not then," he admitted. "But it didn't take long. I began falling in love on our honeymoon—that ridiculous honeymoon. I'm sure you suspected I acted like I did just to get even with you. And it's true. I was angry. Mad about the campaign, mad about having to compromise my life, and yours, just to save face. I had to take my anger out on someone. You were the handiest target, especially when you brought up that ludicrous platonic agreement. I was furious.

"But you were such a damn good sport. It was harder and harder to stay angry. Your spunk. Your loyalty to the campaign. The way Dave and Aunt Sussy and Sam loved you. It all just began sinking in. By the time I came back to New Orleans, I knew I wanted it to be a real marriage."

"Why didn't you tell me?"

"I couldn't. I couldn't trust you. Maybe I've never gotten over my mother walking out on my father, and on me. Trust just isn't a natural feeling for me. I was afraid to let you be around Dave. I was even jealous of Giles sometimes. Mostly I was afraid I'd lose you. After all, I knew you'd only married me to save the campaign. God, Gail, I was so damn frustrated, I didn't know what to do."

He ran his fingers through his hair. "So like a coward, I hid my feelings. And that made me even more miserable.

"Gail, don't leave. I love you. I adore you." His lips pressed against hers urgently, demandingly. Gail returned the kiss, as she wrapped her arms tightly around his neck. The answer he sought was there.

"I'll never leave," she said.

Brad picked her up and carried her toward the bed.

"Brad, they're waiting at campaign headquarters," she murmured.

"Let them wait."

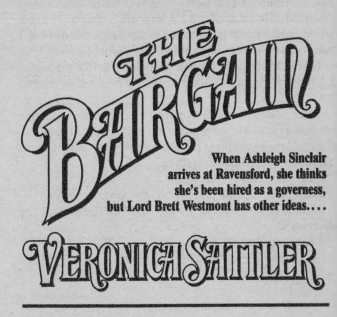

THE BARGAIN

When Ashleigh Sinclair arrives at Ravensford, she thinks she's been hired as a governess, but Lord Brett Westmont has other ideas....

VERONICA SATTLER

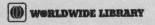

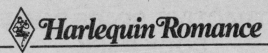
Harlequin Romance

Coming Next Month

2875 THE WAITING HEART Jeanne Allan
City schoolteacher Susan's Christmas holiday at the Colorado ranch of her elderly friend Elizabeth is spoiled by Elizabeth's son—a man who dominates everything and everyone. Expecting to dominate Susan, too, he's surprised by her equally strong resistance!

2876 THE HEART OF THE MATTER Lindsay Armstrong
All her young life Clarry has turned to Robert for help, so it seems entirely natural when he saves her family home by marrying her. Only now there is a price to pay—Clarry has to grow up....

2877 HEARTLAND Bethany Campbell
Budding cartoonist Toby is glad to help temporarily injured top cartoonist Jake Ulrick—but it isn't easy. Cold, abrupt, a tyrant to work for, he resents needing anyone. So it doesn't help matters at all when Toby falls in love with him.

2878 AN ENGAGEMENT IS ANNOUNCED Claudia Jameson
Physiotherapist Anthea Norman cuts short her Canary Islands visit when her hostess's attractive lawyer nephew zooms in for serious pursuit. Instinct tells her to run. She doesn't want to experience the heartbreak of loving and losing again....

2879 SELL ME A DREAM Leigh Michaels
Stephanie has built a career for herself in real estate as well as made a home for her small daughter—the daughter Jordan doesn't know about. And she's practically engaged to staid dependable Tony. Now isn't the time for Jordan to come bouncing back into her life.

2880 NO SAD SONG Alison York
To achieve success in her operatic career, Annabel has to work with Piers Bellingham, the top entrepreneur—and a man she detests. As it turns out, working with Piers is not the problem. It's strictly one of the heart!

Available in December wherever paperback books are sold, or through Harlequin Reader Service.

In the U.S.
901 Fuhrmann Blvd.
P.O. Box 1397
Buffalo, N.Y. 14240-1397

In Canada
P.O. Box 603
Fort Erie, Ontario
L2A 5X3